THE KING AND THE PRINCE

Kingdom of Daes Duo - Book 2

H L MULLER

ISBN: 978-0-6488610-1-0

Cover design by: Avadal Designs
Editing: Salt & Sage Books
Publisher: H. L. Muller

DEDICATION

To the Harrison's and Ambrose's in the world, I hope that you get your fairy tale too.

PROLOGUE

*H*arrison

    A carriage arrived at the luncheon we were hosting for Charming's sixteenth birthday—it was the last garden party of Autumn. I had been pestering Gertrude, trying to rile her up before Prince Charming arrived. Gertrude was obsessed with Charming and talked about him incessantly. Mother only encouraged her—Gertrude had been betrothed to him since she was born, after all.

    That made Gertrude the future queen of Charming's kingdom, just as I was the future king of our kingdom. Everyone expected us to meet a certain standard; we were considered above everyone else and needed to ensure they remembered that fact.

    My chin up, I led Gertrude as we walked over to where Mother and Father were seated beneath a marquee, watching King Kryler and Queen Pomona exit their carriage. Charming stepped out next, followed by a boy I hadn't seen before.

    There was no Ambrose. I didn't care that Ambrose wasn't here; I was actually happy. It meant that I would have more time to be with Charming and not be interrupted by his needy little brother.

    I stared at the new guest and studied his features, absorbed in determining who exactly he was. The longer I looked, the more I noticed how handsome he was.

His clothes were slightly wrinkled from the trip and tight enough that I could make out his toned muscles. He had a sharp jawline and looked to be about the same height as me: five-foot-seven. His shoulder-length black wavy hair was slightly unkempt. I could picture running my hands through it, gripping it and pulling him towards me.

WOAH! What am I thinking! *I could feel my pants growing tighter as I tried to steer my mind within this new territory. He caught my eye and blushed bright pink, captivating me further. His eyes darted away, and, in an attempt to get my thoughts under control, I averted mine as well. The luncheon was going to be hard enough to sit through without a hard-on and feelings I don't understand. I had never thought about men, or women for that matter, this way before and didn't know what it meant.*

"King Kryler, Queen Pomona, Prince Charming, and Prince Ambrose, sir." The butler introduced the party.

My eyes shot back to the unknown boy—he was Ambrose? It was not possible?! Ambrose was short and always had his head buried in a book. I studied him further, and on closer inspection confirmed that it was Ambrose. He had just changed a lot since the last time I had seen him.

Mother sat Ambrose and I next to each other, ensuring that Gertrude had 'alone' time with Charming. It was hard to be disgruntled by this now as my reward was 'alone' time with Ambrose. At first, I was nervous and could barely get any words out of my mouth. I realised I didn't know Ambrose very well as I had never spent the time to get to know him.

Leaping into a conversation, I said, "If we are going to get through this luncheon, I think we need to have an engaging conversation. Please, tell me something interesting?"

"Fine," Ambrose said. "What is interesting to you?"

I looked at him and made eye-contact—he had extraordinary pale blue eyes.

"Wow, you are beautiful," I muttered—I couldn't help it, the words just came out of me without permission. I felt my cheeks heat in embarrassment and glanced away waiting for Ambrose's reproach.

He stared at me as if I had just slapped him across the face. He swallowed, and then he whispered, "You think I am beautiful?" There wasn't disgust in his voice—there was awe.

Deciding to be honest, I replied, "I suppose I do."

He laughed deep and breathy, and it lit me up inside.

"Something interesting, hmm," he said, thankfully changing the subject back to my earlier question. "With Charming next in line for the throne, it is likely that I will end up as an advisor on his council. So, instead, I have decided to become a knight."

That shocked me; he had never come across as a violent person at all, always more into books.

"Well, if you don't want to be an advisor, you could be an academic," I offered.

"No, it's not something I can do." His eyes flicked to his father, and I understood. It wasn't a matter of ability; it was a matter of permission.

"I imagine that becoming a knight will take a lot of work, right?" I asked, moving the conversation on to not cause him any more discomfort.

"Oh, you have no idea!"

We spent the rest of the luncheon discussing the training, trials, and commitments that he would need to undertake to become a knight. He didn't know all the details, but he had spoken to a knight in his father's guard and had a good idea of what to expect.

After the luncheon, Mother took us all on a walk around the gardens, an excuse to prolong Charming's time with Gertrude.

Ambrose and I walked side by side, our shoulders bumping, and then our hands occasionally brushing. I felt my skin break flush every time we made contact.

* * *

The jolt of the carriage brought me out of my memories, alerting me that we had arrived at the castle where Ambrose lived with his family. Nerves course through me, as I knew I would be alone with him tonight. I have been drawn to him for the last five years—since I first noticed him at that luncheon, and it never diminished. I felt whole when I was with Ambrose. My yearning for him grows stronger each time we are apart. I haven't seen him in a few months; he was off on another quest that I am almost certain he was using as an excuse to be away from his Father.

It is stupid. I needed to look for a wife; there could be no future between him and me, no matter how drawn to him I am.

I step down from our carriage and enter the castle, glad that, for once, Mother and Father were more absorbed in Gertrude this evening. I stand next to her, my eyes flicking around the grand room, taking in the chandeliers, food, and decorations set up for tonight's ball. Today we are celebrating Prince Charming's twenty-first birthday and announcing Charming and Gertrude's engagement.

We had barely arrived, and I hardly had time to make eye-contact with Ambrose across the room, when Charming opened the ball, dancing with a strange woman and escorting her out to the gardens.

I had expected Charming and Gertrude to be absorbed in each other all night, so I am shocked. Gertrude is now left alone and free to keep an eye on me if she wanted. I couldn't have that; Ambrose and I have been carving out secret moments together for so long now it has turned into a routine, and tonight was too important to let Gertrude ruin it.

"Snubbed were you, Sister dear? Did you even get the chance to speak with him? What is to happen with you now?" I ask quietly. Without a response, Gertrude storms off. I counted on that reaction, and hopefully, she'll avoid me the rest of the night.

To keep up appearances and to keep Mother off my back, I dance with a young woman whose name I didn't care to ask. When the song ended, I rotated through a few more dance part-ners, not showing them any care or interest, but spending the time to show my parents that I am indeed looking for a wife and trying my hardest to meet someone suitable. As I work my way around the room, my eyes follow Ambrose, tracking his movements as he also shares a few dances and enjoys the festivities.

Ambrose catches my eye briefly before slipping outside. It is our chance to spend some time together—having spent enough time creating a presence in the party, no one will notice that we stepped out. I loiter at a table filled with desserts and sweet treats for five minutes. Then I sneak out of the ballroom too.

Walking along the lighted path, I withdraw a cigarette and light it. I am not a smoker; it's a front to escape from functions. I reached the edge of the hedge maze where Ambrose and I often escaped to meet.

I enter it, and my steps were strong and sure. I take the turns that lead me to the centre, and finally, see my handsome Ro sitting there on a stone bench expectantly. He is in a navy-blue suit that stretches across his broad shoulders, his sky-blue eyes heating as they meet mine. I don't stop walking until I am directly in front of him, hooking my hand under his chin. I bend down as he reaches up, and our lips meet in a searing hot kiss.

Ambrose is fractionally taller than me and the seating arrangement allows me the chance to be above him for once. Taking advantage of the position, I push his body back slightly and, without breaking the kiss, I straddle his lap. His tongue moves in my mouth, playing with mine and tasting me. My hands shift from his jaw, sliding down to his chest and twisting into his shirt.

"I missed you so much, Baby." His breath caresses my mouth. Sparks tingle down my spine, reaching out to the tips of my fingers and toes. I shiver at the feeling. Ambrose grins; he knows what calling me Baby does to me. That's why he does it whenever he gets the chance.

A moan escapes me, too captivated by him to find any words, my hands trail down the long muscular length of his torso, feeling his muscles through his shirt tense under my touch. My hand drops and palm the tent in his pants. Not wanting to waste a second of our limited time, so I undo his pants and snake my hand inside, wrapping it around his long, hard, thick cock. Ambrose groans, thrusting his hips instinctively into my warm and familiar hand.

"You can't have all the fun, Baby." He murmurs, sliding his hands down my back and landing on my ass. Gripping my cheeks and pulling my body closer, he growls low in appreciation. "Mine, Harrison, this ass, this body, you, are mine," He whispered into my ear.

I threw my head back and moaned. His declaration, combined with his seductive voice, is winding me up, and he knows it. Ambrose has never claimed me outright before, and with the way he was kissing down my throat, I am close to cumming in my pants.

Knowing what I need, Ambrose moves his hands around to undo my pants, pulling my length out and stroking me gently. He brings his lips back to mine, and I lose myself in the feeling of his tongue, exploring my mouth. But it isn't enough. I break the kiss and pull back enough to make eye contact with him.

"I need to taste you, Ro. I need to feel you in my mouth, sliding down my throat." I whisper, knowing too well he cannot resist me. He nods, and I take pleasure at rendering him speechless. I climb off his lap, a soft protest falling from his lips fades into a groan as my mouth envelops his cock.

I look up to check his expression and see him staring down at me. Maintaining eye contact, I slide my mouth up and down his throbbing cock. Using my hands, I massage his balls and jerk my cock. We were both on the edge of cumming, and I feel regret flash through me: sad that we don't have more time to tease and draw out our time together. We are risking a lot by being together tonight—anyone from the ball could walk out into the gardens and find us.

Ambrose's hands twist into my long, chocolate brown hair. I

had learned that he loved not only the look of it but using it as a handhold. I had left it unbound purely for him tonight. He simultaneously holds my hair from my face and pushes me down on his cock as he starts fucking my mouth.

My orgasm catches me off guard—I explode onto the gravel floor. As I cum, I suck Ambrose harder and deeper into my throat, moaning through my release. Ambrose's cock swells and throbs in my mouth, "Shit, Baby... I'm goin..." His voice breaks off, holding my face down as he thrusts into my mouth a final time before cumming. I swallow around his length, savouring the salty taste.

"Oh yes, Baby, swallow my cum." He groans, watching me pull him from my mouth. I flick my tongue over his head to capture every last drop and lick my lips. I show him my empty mouth. Ambrose uses his hold on my hair to pull me back up to his lap, and our lips meet in another passionate kiss. His mouth is warm, treating me with reverence and tenderness.

Alternating between soft and deep kisses, I gently return our now softening cocks back inside our pants and straighten both our clothing. I pull back reluctantly and climb off Ambrose's lap.

"I've missed you, Ro. You were away so long this time; where did you go? Your father did not mention it when they came for dinner last week." I sigh and sit down next to Ambrose on the stone bench.

"Father sent me off into the Kingdom of the Green Eves. He is hoping that I will select a bride from among their nobility to ensure we have a connection and alliance with another strong Kingdom." I tense. The thought of him marrying someone else causes jealousy and pain to course through me. If he notices my reaction, he doesn't mention it. Steeling myself and shuttering my emotions, I avoid looking at him.

"Did you find someone suitable then? Is that why you returned? Are we celebrating your marriage soon after Charming and Gertrude's?" I can hear the intensity in my voice.

"What do you want me to say to that, Harry? You know I want to be with you, but you are out there flirting with women and searching for a wife! How hypocritical of you. You are in the same position as me." His hand reaches out and cups my face, forcing me to look at him. Then he brushes his thumb over my cheek before letting his hand fall back to his lap. "Besides, I didn't go."

"What?"

"I didn't go to the Kingdom of Green Eves; I said Father sent me there, not that I went. I was off in the Jang Forest, exploring and getting to know the way around."

"You have to be careful in the Jang Forest, Ro. The Silent Wood could snatch you up." Panic seizes me; I can't lose him. "Promise me you won't go back into the Jang Forest, please?"

"I wish I could, Baby, but I am a knight—I have to go where I am needed, even if that puts me at risk. Besides, I never put any stock into that myth. I'm certain The Silent Wood was made up by husbands not wanting to return to their wives."

I nod. I understand what Ambrose is saying, but that doesn't mean I have to like it.

"Harrison, there's something I want to talk to you about," he says. I study his face and take in his grim yet determined expression. He rarely calls me Harrison when we are alone, and I have a gut feeling that this is not going to be a pleasant conversation. I nod, not trusting my voice.

"I want to be with you, for real. Out in the open, to have everyone know that I am yours and that you are mine. To be able to call you my husband, my king, to grow old with you. I don't want you to get a wife—I want you to give us a chance."

"No."

I say it before I realise I even planned to. I feel like someone else is using my body as a puppet, and I feel out of control. I'm a heartbroken bystander watching my whole world crumble to pieces.

The words he said caused an image to form. I see it, us ruling side by side, me seeing him every day, holding him, cherishing him, experiencing life with him. I crave it, and I need it to be true. I dreamt of these things before, secretly longing for them for years. But they couldn't be real. I am a future king, I cannot come out, I cannot be with a man, it is not possible, and he knows that.

"I-I-I can't, Ambrose. It can't happen."

His forlorn expression cuts me.

"You can't tell me you don't feel this between us, Harry. I know you do! You are the love of my life! I cannot even remember what my life was like before you. You are my best friend, my companion; I know you feel the same as I do. Why can't you give us a chance?" His voice breaks, "Why can't we come out to our families and make our wishes known? I don't care if they cast me out or abandon me; I will be happy as long as I have you in my life."

"You don't get it! I CAN'T!" I yell. First, I remember the other guests and the possibility of getting caught, and then I realise he just said he loves me for the first time. Maybe he didn't mean it. I lower my voice. "You know it's not possible! Why would you put me in this position?"

I can't believe how selfish he is being. How could he not understand that I want this, want him, and the pretty future he painted for us? Yet I couldn't have it. I couldn't be a king with a husband.

We often had conversations across dinner tables and crowded rooms through eye contact alone. Tonight, his eyes are begging me to give in to him, asking me to allow us both to be happy.

"I can't, Ambrose, I am sorry, but I just can't. I don't see any way that we would be allowed to be together."

"You know I would do anything for you, right, Baby? I love you."

My breath hitches in my throat, not allowing me to respond. There it is again, those three words. Ambrose leans forward and kisses me. He doesn't stop until I am panting for breath again.

Separating from each other is hard, but we pull back and, knowing our time is up, begin walking back through the maze holding hands. We savour the cover of the hedges before we head back into the ball.

"Just think about it, ok?" He brings my hand to his mouth and places a lingering kiss. With no more talk between us, we drop hands and walk in different directions toward the ball.

I re-enter the ballroom and glance at the clock, surprised to see there are only five minutes until midnight. I had not realised how much time we spent in the maze. I walked the edges of the room, taking stock of the guests, checking if anyone was paying too much attention to me. Thankfully, no one appears to be looking for me and my extended absence wasn't noticed. Across the room, Gertrude is without Charming, standing only with our parents. I don't know if he had returned, or what was going on, but I doubted they announced the engagement if she looks that miserable.

Without realising, I had walked up to the door where Ambrose is re-joining the party. As we lock eyes, he offers me a small smile; to anyone else, he looks happy and normal. I could see the pain lingering underneath, and it hurts me to see it and to know I caused it.

We were friends, and everyone would expect us to talk to each other. I turn to him and act the part.

"Prince Ambrose, where is that brother of yours? Isn't he meant to be with Gertrude? Announcing something?" Raising my eyebrow with the question.

Ambrose's eyes widen as he looks around the room, shock all over his face. He hadn't noticed that his brother was missing either—the clock chimes midnight, which cuts off his response to my question. I am about to turn to join my family when the Mystery Woman that Charming was dancing with earlier runs into the room. The music stops, and guests fall silent as we watch her bolt up the stairs and out of the ballroom.

Charming follows at her heels. "Wait! Don't go!" Charming calls after her.

"What is happening?" I say to Ambrose, but when I turn, there's an empty spot where he was standing. Looking up, I see him across the room, following his father out of the ballroom.

Chapter One

HARRISON

Three Months Later

Everything went to shit after Prince Charming's birthday. Charming married Cinderella, leaving Gertrude to be showcased around like she is a prize to be won. There were even painful talks of her marrying Ambrose before Father *thankfully* shut it down.

The thought of him on top of her in bed made me crazy with jealousy—I had held off on us doing the same. I wanted our first time to be somewhere we didn't have to be careful about how much noise we made or about who else could be walking around the garden beds and could catch us. I wanted the time to savour his body and enjoy the pleasure I know he would bring to mine. It has also been three months since I have heard from Ambrose. I spent the winter months writing letters to him and throwing them away, unable to find the right words. Normally, we write letters to each other and maintain contact while we're apart. This time, I don't know how to reach out to him after our conversation at the ball. I still don't see a way that we can be together and be accepted. I know he wants us to be together, and I want that too, but I know my duty to be king of this king-dom. I need to produce heirs. I could not fathom the kingdom's reaction if they knew that I was gay and thinking about getting in bed with a man. I hadn't even admitted it aloud to myself.

I know it is unfair to keep him hanging. I wish I could be daring like Ambrose. Able to put my deepest desires out there and just hope for the best. I should be braver. I have been afraid of people finding out since our first kiss.

The thought brings the memory back to me. It had been the first of many stolen kisses and moments that we would go on to share.

Since the luncheon for Charming's sixteenth birthday, we had formed a friendship based around fondness and attraction. I was just hoping that I wasn't misreading his signals. We were hosting a dinner one night, and I took a moment to steal Mother's attention.

"Mother, may we be excused, so can I take Ambrose to the library, please? There's something I want to show him."

Mother was all too happy to wave us on our way; we were not her main focus with Charming and Gertrude under her watchful gaze, and Ambrose and I quickly left the room. Anticipation coursed through me as we walked down the hallways alone, no guards or maids in sight. Taking a leap of faith, I grasp Ambrose's hand. Gripping it tightly, I pull him down the hallway and into the library. I didn't let go as we entered the empty library. I was sometimes in the library at any hour of the night; I knew the librarian left in the mid-afternoon, the maids would not be back until the early hours of the morning, and the guard would not do a walk-through for a few hours.

"What did you want to show me, Harry?" Ro asked, his brows furrowed..

"This," I replied brazenly, cupping his face and kissing him on the mouth. It was my first kiss and his, too; I knew that from our endless conversations over the last year. As I pulled back, Ambrose's hands reached up and twisted into my shirt, pulling my body back to his, and putting his lips back onto mine.

Mother and Father paraded Gertrude and I around for the last three months in the vain attempt to marry us off. We hosted many dinner parties and had noblemen and women from all over the kingdom stay for weekends. I had women throwing themselves at me every other day, hoping to seduce me. The reality was that none of them wanted *me; they* wanted a chance at a crown. Their efforts were futile; I only wanted Ambrose.

We are expecting Lady Lucy from the House of the Claw today. I am dreading it. I had reached a point where I didn't know what to do anymore. I can't see the path forward: I can't be with Ambrose, and I can't marry a woman. I just want to avoid the whole world.

In an attempt to forget about my worries and distract myself, I go in search of Gertrude. She is usually either in her rooms or in the garden at this time of the day. It is cruel of me, but I enjoy toying with her to distract me from my problems. I had been doing it for so long that it was hard to stop now.

I had always been jealous of Gertrude. She had everything I wanted, no longer in line for a throne, the freedom to be herself, and no one would bat an eye if the offer for her to marry Ambrose went through.

I knock on Gertrude's bedroom door and receive no response. Letting myself in, I look around and couldn't see any sign of her, Evalyn, or any ladies' maids. She must be in the gardens then, all the better for distracting myself with a walk in our mini-wood. Venturing out into the gardens, I notice the strange lack of guards or servers that I encounter. Were these halls usually this empty? I would have thought Gertrude's wing would be more protected than this.

I knew most of Gertrude's usual haunts in the gardens and took the paths to all of them. After walking around for an hour, I saw no trace of Gertrude anywhere. Things are starting to get suspicious. Where could she be?

The stables! Of course, how stupid of me to not think about checking the stables! Turning quickly on my heel, I walk to the palace stables on the other side of the garden, still keeping an eye out to find Gertrude.

The stables were deserted empty when I got there with no

stable hands or workers around. I walk to the stall where Gertrude's horse Stormy stays. Empty. Stormy, her saddle, and Gertrude are all gone. What is going on? I look around, and still, I could not see anyone.

"HELLO?" I call out into the attached barn.

"Oh! Just a moment!" A deep voice calls out.

A moment later, a man shuffles out of the barn, looking very ruffled. His short brown hair is all messed about, and his brown linen shirt is untucked from his trousers, which he is in the process of tying up. If I didn't know better, I would say I interrupted him in the middle of masturbating. But I knew better, right?

"How can I help you today?" he says without looking at me, too distracted with doing up his pants.

"Your Highness," I respond. If I can't make Gertrude's day miserable, perhaps this man could be an adequate substitute.

His eyes snap to me immediately, "I am sorry, Your Highness! I was not aware that it was you. How may I assist you today?"

I smirk at him—I always enjoy it when peasants fell over themselves to fawn over royals and high-ranking noblemen, and he is proving to be entertaining.

"The Princess, have you seen her? I can see that Stormy is not here. Did Princess Gertrude take her out for a ride with Evalyn?"

"No, Your Highness. Evalyn did not go with her. When I came in this morning, Stormy was already gone; the stable boy told me that Princess Gertrude left at dawn to take her out for a ride."

"Alone?"

"I believe so, Your Highness."

"Why was she alone? Is the king aware?"

"We were ordered by the princess not to speak up until someone came looking for her. She told the stable boy she would be back before three in the afternoon."

"Right, well, in the future, ensure that Evalyn or the King is aware of her movements! She can't be going out alone. We have just broken ties with King Kryler; who knows what could happen to her out there." I walk out of the stable door to inspect the sundial in the courtyard. It is well past four in the afternoon. I stalk back into the stables; the man was still standing there, stunned.

"By your account of what has happened, she should have been back almost two hours ago. So, where is she?"

His face pales, the gravity of the situation starting to sink in. His mouth opens and closes as he tries to find something that I will want to hear.

"Which direction did she go? Did she tell the stable boy where she was going?"

The man still has no answers.

"Get me the stable boy!" I bark out the order.

I watch and wait as the man scrambles out the stable door and runs in the direction of their quarters. How stupid can these people be? She is a princess for crying out loud. She can't just gallivant across the countryside alone.

"Your Highness, what are you doing down here?" Evalyn's voice breaks my train of thought, and I turn around to look at her.

"I think the more accurate question, Evalyn, is what are you doing here? And why were you not with Gertrude?"

As she opens her mouth to respond, the man rushes back into the stable, a boy in tow. It hits me then that Evalyn has appeared from the barn and not the front entrance. I take a moment to study her appearance; she looked as she always did, elegant in a long flowing dress until I noticed the hay in her hair.

"Were you to busy fucking to notice Gertrude is gone?!" I roar.

"Well... no, I-I was looking for her." She replies meekly, tucking her chin.

An act I have seen her play before, not having the patience to handle her now—I turn to the stable boy. "Where did she go?"

"I don't know, Your Highness. I saw her go into the Jang Forest, and that was it," the boy replies, cowering slightly under my gaze.

"And why did you not alert anyone that she had left, alone might I add?"

"She ordered me not to, Your Highness. She was very explicit that I was only to tell the household if they asked where she was."

How curious. Why would Gertrude make such a strange order? She wasn't trying to hide that she was going at all; she just didn't want anyone to know until they were too late. Mother and Father barely notice us these days outside of trying to find us both 'suitable' bed-mates. Was this a cry for attention?

"I want you to stay here and wait for her return; please send for me directly the moment she does. I will be speaking with the King regarding this matter."

As I leave the stables and walk directly back into the palace, I notice one of the guards, Joseph, on duty.

Walking up to him, I say, "Joseph, where is the king? And did you know Gertrude was out?"

"He is in his study, my Prince. I did not know she was out. Is Evalyn with her?"

I set off walking towards my Father's study, Joseph following and keeping pace with me. "No, she went out alone."

"Alone? Sir, how long has she been out?"

"According to the man in the stables, she left at dawn and intended to return before three this afternoon. She hasn't returned."

We arrive at Father's study. I knock and wait.

"Enter!" He barks out, his voice loud enough to project across the room and through the heavy wooden door.

Joseph opens the door for me, allowing me to enter first before closing the door behind us.

"Ah, Harrison, my boy! What brings you to see me today? It's almost time for dinner with Lady Lucy. I do hope you were there to greet her when she arrived this afternoon!" Father spoke in such a cheery voice; I felt awful that I was about to ruin his good mood. I had forgotten entirely about Lady Lucy arriving.

"Gertrude is gone, Father. She went out for a ride on Stormy at dawn this morning and has not returned. She told the stable boy that she would be back by three. It is now close to five, and she has not made an appearance." I say hastily, anxious to break the news as quickly as possible.

"I'm sure Evalyn and the guards that went with her will have it all under control, son. You must get ready for dinner."

"Father—"

"Now, Harrison," he cut me off, "you need to start getting ready now. Gertrude will be along when she is along. Tonight is for you, not for her."

"But, Father—"

"ENOUGH! You obey me, Harrison. Now leave—go and prepare for dinner. Joseph, please escort him back to his rooms at once!"

I knew my face showed pure anger at my Father. He wouldn't even listen to me. But I knew I could not reason with him when he was like this.

I storm out of the room, slamming the door open on my way into the hallway. Taking my anger at the situation out on the palace seemed like a good idea. I could hear Joseph follow me out, and I ignored him until I reached my sitting room. I spun around to him.

"You need to keep a look out for her. I have already told the stable boy that I am to be alerted when she returns. Without alerting the King, have the guards look in the Jang Forest, he saw her head in that direction."

"Of course, my prince. Should the stable boy be punished for not alerting us to her departure earlier?"

"As much as I would like to, I fear that he is not at fault. He was following Gertrude's orders, which is what we ask servants to do. He should have known better and told someone, but it's not like there was a sign saying, *Gertrude can only leave with a guard and her governess.* Speaking of, we need to find out why Evalyn wasn't with Gertrude. Speak with the stable master—find out what happened."

"Yes, my prince, I will do that while you attend the dinner," Joseph smirks. I flip him off on my way to the bathroom. He knows how much I hate women being flaunted to me like they're prized cattle; he's the only one in the palace who knows my secret. We had always been good friends, and I knew I could trust him. He had even helped run interference when I snuck off for time with Ambrose.

It may have been improper, but I had chambermaids who helped me groom and dress, rather than a valet. I can't stand the thought of getting aroused while being washed or dressed by a hot young man. When I hit puberty and demanded women bathe me, they flaunted their goods and "accidentally" spilled water over their white linen blouses, turning them transparent. It did nothing for me, and after a few months of no response, they eventually got the idea and left it to just cleaning me.

After a quick bath, I dressed and sought out Joseph, who was in the main entrance hallway, no doubt waiting for me on the way to the main sitting room. I wanted to get to the bottom of the situation with Gertrude.

"Any news?" I continue walking past Joseph, and he falls into step walking with me towards the sitting room.

"Nothing, my prince. She has not returned. Guards are still patrolling the Jang Forest main path. I have sent men to go into villages and ask after her. Another guard is speaking to everyone in the main market to see if anyone saw what direction she headed in."

"And Evalyn?"

"The stable master confirmed he was... physically engaged with her when you arrived," Joseph answers modestly. "Apparently, they have been satisfying each other's sexual appetites for a short while now. She always seeks him out when she has need of him. He is not permitted to find her."

I cringed, and my lip curls up in disgust. Joseph grins at my reaction, seeming to take pleasure in causing me discomfort.

"Please notify me the moment you hear any word of Gertrude. I don't know what it is, but this situation feels off. My gut is telling me something went wrong. Interrupt dinner if you have to; let me know the moment she gets back or when the guards return."

"Of course, my prince." Joseph bows slightly while opening the sitting room door for me. Mother and Father are the only people present so far. At least I arrived before Lady Lucy. I could not bear the lecture I would inevitably receive from Mother if I had arrived after the "guest of honour."

"Evening Mother," I place a kiss on her cheek. "Evening Father," I shake his hand and bow my head slightly. "Any word from Gertrude?"

"Gertrude? What do you mean, Harrison?" Mother asks, eyes flicking between Father and me.

Father interrupts before I have a chance to inform Mother of the situation. "I'm sure she will be along shortly, she knows her duty." I fight to not to roll my eyes. He is really beyond reasoning if he could not even listen to his crown prince. He will find out soon enough that Gertrude is gone; Evalyn will arrive and bring it to his attention. It is her job to be aware of Gertrude's whereabouts and to babysit her at all times.

As if I summoned her with my thought, Evalyn enters the room without Gertrude. However, she did have Lady Lucy follow her in.

"Good evening, ladies, how are we all this pleasant evening?" My father asks.

"Good evening, I am well, my king." They reply in unison while curtsying to him.

This whole show is starting to piss me off. How stupid can

my own family be? Does no one notice that Gertrude wasn't here?

"Since we are all here now, shall we go through for dinner?" my mother says.

"All here?" I laugh. "Where is Gertrude, Evalyn?"

Four sets of shocked eyes all dart around the room, as if Gertrude is hiding somewhere, before flicking between myself and Evalyn.

"I do not know; she hasn't returned yet, Your Highness," she replies while a soft scowl distorts her features. She clearly doesn't want me to bring attention to this.

"What do you mean, Evalyn? I don't understand. You let her go out without you?" Shock laces my mother's voice.

"*I* didn't let her do anything." Evalyn murmurs, "She left the palace at dawn this morning, Your Majesties, and has not yet returned."

"Why are you only telling us this now?" My father roars, his face boiling red.

"Prince Harrison was meant to tell you, my king," Evalyn smirks as she glances over at me. That bitch is trying to make it out to be my fault. How petty and classless of her. Obviously, she forgot she was at fault and that I know everything.

I jump in before Mother or Father had the chance to turn on me. "Father, I tried to tell you hours ago, and you weren't listening. I already have guards out looking for her, Joseph is keeping me updated, and currently, there is no sign of her. The only thing we know is that she headed in the direction of the Jang Forest and informed the stable boy she would be back before three in the afternoon. What I would like to know, however, is why Evalyn was not aware of her whereabouts until I alerted her to Gertrude's absence around four. Evalyn?"

Evalyn turns a bright shade of pink while scowling at me. It is an odd look.

"Never mind that now!" Father begins pacing the room, "We need to find Gertrude before anyone hears that she is gone. If it gets out that she is too headstrong, or worse, is no longer virtuous, we will lose any hope of an advantageous marriage. We were expecting Lord Damien to return from the Kingdom of Eves next week to finalise his engagement with Gertrude. We need the arrangement with him to go ahead to solidify our alliance—our trades have been lacking since I cut ties off with King Kryler."

I shake my head in shock and horror.

"She is missing—Why are you only worried about the potential marriage with Lord Damien and not her safety?"

As if he didn't hear me, he continues, "It must have been King Kryler and Prince Charming. I would bet my life they have her. Cynthia," he says as he turns to my mother, "we must act. We need to get our daughter back before she ruins this family."

Father stalks out of the room without another glance in my direction; Evalyn and Mother follow dutifully behind him. I turn to Lady Lucy, who my parents had forgotten about in the fray. "I am sorry we did not expect this to happen. I hate to cut your stay here short, but I think it would be best if you left in the morning. We have a lot to handle here, as I am sure you surmised."

"I could help you, Your Highness?" It is the first time I heard her voice—squeaky and annoying. I can't imagine having to listen to her for a moment longer, let alone the rest of my life.

"No, that's alright, Lady Lucy. It is a family matter that we need to settle. I will ensure there are arrangements for your departure in the morning. If you could please keep the information to yourself, for the time being, we will arrange for your return here as soon as everything settles."

I kiss her hand in farewell and leave the room, giving orders on the way out for Joseph to arrange Lady Lucy's departure and have her dinner brought to her room.

Chapter Two

AMBROSE

Dear Prince Ambrose,
I have to discuss something urgent with you
in person. Please meet me at my favourite
place in my palace garden tomorrow at noon.
Sincerely,
Prince Harrison

It is the first I have heard from Harry in months, and it is oddly formal. In our previous letters, he wouldn't use any titles, using Ro and Harry, not our full names. Since my brother's birthday celebration, since I asked him if we could be together for real, I have not heard from him until now, and the formality in his letter tells me something is wrong. Every day I mentally battle with myself, arguing if I should reach out and talk to him. I told him to think about it and don't want to sway him or make the decision for him, but the silence since Charming's ball has led me to assume that he is working himself up to breaking everything off with me.

I have heard about dinner parties and weekend visitors. He will need to make a decision soon. His parents will push a bride and future queen on him, and he will probably accept. That's what he told me at the ball, wasn't it?

So why this letter now? Letters had been our most common communication method over the last five years. They were usually in code, asking for me to meet him somewhere private for us to "talk." This letter is the first time I hoped that talking is actually what he us wants to do.

I put it all on the table for Harry months ago, sick of us not being able to be ourselves, to be with each other openly. We are young, yes, but I know he is it for me. I knew from our first kiss that he would be my everything, from our touches and secret caresses under the dining table to exploring each other's bodies and discovering our fantasies and pleasures. We are a perfect pair.

Now here I am, sitting at the small lake in the palace gardens after sneaking in, waiting for Harry to show. When we met in private previously, Harry thought it was better if no one in the palace knew I was here. It would help keep our relationship a secret if no one suspected me of visiting too often, so I came while I was supposed to be off on a quest or journey.

I know he is scared. I know he's not ashamed of me, but sometimes it felt like I'm his dirty little secret that he keeps hidden in the closet. At the same time, he has a different woman on his arm every other week to keep up appearances.

Stop it, Ambrose! You are overthinking things again. You know that Harrison loves you—well, he never said it, remember? Stop!

I was pacing along the lake's edge when he arrived, appearing beneath a large oak tree I had once pressed him into; it was the first time I got down on my knees and worshipped his cock with my mouth. The thought of that day has me hardening in my pants.

Without thinking, I step into his personal space and push him further into the tree. The need to touch him consumes me as it always does after being separated from him. All my mind and body can focus on is being in his arms again, to feel him and know he is there. I drag my fingers down the side of his face, and without words, lean down and kiss him. The moment his lips touch mine, the knots in my chest start to unfurl. I am at peace whenever I am in his embrace, and it has been too long since I had touched him.

Pulling back, so our lips are only just touching, I whisper, "I've missed you, Baby."

"I've missed you too, Ro," he whispers too. I am afraid to break the moment of reconnection, fearful that I will ruin everything if I start asking questions. So instead, I kiss him softly again, before pulling him over to sit on the bench seat with me. I wait in silence, relishing having his hand in mine, the softness of his thumb brushing over my hard calluses.

He summoned me here, so he obviously had something he wanted to do or discuss. I am an open book with him, and he knows that. He's staring out at the lake with a solemn expression, avoiding my gaze.

"Gertrude has been missing for three days," He begins. "She went on a ride by herself at dawn on the first day of Spring and never returned. Evalyn didn't keep a close enough eye on her and didn't realise she was missing until four in the afternoon. She was too *busy*."

I am speechless. From all the thoughts I built up about this meeting in my mind, this had not been one of them. Not knowing how to respond, I watch Harry as he struggles to continue.

"Father is adamant that Charming has her." He finally looks at me. "Or that someone in your family does."

"What?" I laugh, jumping up from the bench. "You think that we have kidnapped her?"

"Father won't waver. He thinks that this is your family retaliating for him cutting ties and allegiance. Since Father was about to announce Gertrude's engagement to Lord Damien of the Kingdom of Eves, he has convinced everyone at court that one of you have stolen her in revenge."

I cannot keep up with this and resume my earlier pacing, "So, just to be sure that I understand this properly, Gertrude has gone off on a day adventure alone and didn't return, and the first thought is that we kidnapped her?"

"Yes," his jaw tenses, a sign that he is getting angry.

"We don't have her. Why would we take her?" I reply bluntly.

"How do you know?" He asks, ignoring my question.

I stop in my tracks and twist to face him, "Is my word not good enough? Can't you just believe me? They are my family, I know them, I know they don't have her! If you need our help—my help—in finding her, I can organise that. But I am telling you now—we don't have her!"

"How can you be sure? Charming or your father could have her and be hiding it from you. Can't you at least go and ask them to be certain?"

"They don't have her! Why won't you trust me?" I don't have the strength to mask the pain in my voice. My beloved does not believe me.

"Why are you being so difficult!? This is my sister we are talking about!"

"You hate Gertrude! Why do you suddenly care about her now?"

"I-I-." He stammers, anger contorting his face, "Are you doing this because I said no? Because I want to keep our relationship a secret?"

"Do you really think I would kidnap your sister because you want to keep me your dirty little secret?" I can feel my heart fracturing in my chest—how can my sweet Harry think I am capable of such things?

"It's possible you could be doing this to get back at me, yes, or using it as leverage to manipulate me into a public relationship."

"Manipulate," I parrot on a breath—Did this man not know me at all? "I knew nothing of her disappearance until you called me here today. My family and I did not steal her away with the hope of blackmailing you or your family." I hate myself—hate him—for needing to justify myself, "Father and Charming do not even know that I am gay, because you need me to keep it a secret for you. I do not think that I was being unreasonable when I asked you to take our relationship further. I love you, for fuck's sake!"

"I love you too, Ro! Can't you see how hard this is for me? See my position? I am the heir to the throne; I can't be gay."

"Except for the fact that you are gay, Harrison. The amount of time we have spent kissing and loving each other is a pretty huge indicator of that!" Glossing over the confession of his love.

"I just can't, Ro."

"So that is your decision? After all this time spent together, after what I said at the ball, you are saying no?"

"I don't want to say no, but I can't say yes."

"Then, I need to leave now. Can I ask for a final kiss goodbye?"

"Final?" He asks, tears welling at the corner of his eyes—this is hurting him as much as it is me.

"You are saying no, Baby." I say, as calm as I can be in the face of my heart shattering, "This is it; I can't keep doing this. Sneaking around and not being able to claim you as mine is not enough for me anymore. We are both adults now, with responsibilities. I thought we had a future together, and I thought we would be together forever. If you are saying no, then you need to let me go so I can move on and have the life that I deserve to have."

A tear escapes and slips down Harry's cheek, and he ignores it as he walks to me and cups my face.

"I am sorry, Ro. I will always love you." His lips press against mine in a searing kiss. The salt of his tears invades our kiss as they continue to fall, and I know I will never get the taste out of my mouth. His kiss is possessive and violent, and our tongues dance around each other, his teeth biting into my lip.

"Ahem!" a soft feminine voice breaks our connection; we

hastily pull away from each other and try to look like we were not making out. "Well, well. What do we have here, Prince Harrison?" Evalyn speaks in a singsong voice.

For five years we have never been caught, and now that we are over, we are at risk of the world finding out. Sometimes fate is cruel. As much as I want us to be out, it can't happen like this: forced into a corner and being outed by someone else. We both stand there speechless; I can see Harry's face contort with pain as if he is going to be sick.

"Evalyn, wh-what are you doing here?" Harry blurts out.

"Me? I would much rather know what the two of you are doing here. This man is from an enemy kingdom, Harrison. How do you think your father would respond to that?"

"M-my father?" Harrison is in shock, the wheels turning in his mind as he tries to process the situation.

"Yes, I am sure he will be furious when he hears about this. Unless he doesn't find out, that is."

"What do you want from us?" I ask. I don't care about her knowing about me, but I hate the position this is putting Harry in. He just stated that he didn't want to come out, and now, here in a private moment, when he was in his favourite place, someone found out.

"Nothing from you, Ambrose. I do not care about you, but Harrison here. I think there is something he can do for me that will prevent me from speaking about this with the King."

"What do you want?" he growls.

"Didn't you hear? The King removed me from the court. Since that was your fault, you are to convince the King that I will stay on, by any means necessary. If I am removed from this palace, then the whole world will know what you are."

Chapter Three

AMBROSE

Harrison agreed. Of course, he agreed. Harrison made it clear he could not cope with anyone knowing he is gay or someone outing him to his family, court, and kingdom. He left me standing there in the garden, watching him walk away with that awful woman. Harrison dismissed me in the same breath that accepted Evalyn's *offer*—proving with his actions that he would rather have Evalyn manipulate him than consider being with me for his happiness.

I understand—or at least I think I understand—why he feels like he needs to keep his sexuality a secret. I have experienced some of the same pressure and expectations that Harrison has. But I think he is worth any controversy. Clearly, he does not feel the same about me.

Doubt fills me thinking over our time spent together, now tainted by arguments and pain. Had he actually wanted to be with me? Or was I just someone to fool around with when he started to discover his sexuality? He had been quick to stop me, declining my offer for more.

I berate myself, *Stop it! Now is not the time for such thoughts!*

I ride home as fast as my horse, Onyx, can carry me, catching sight of the Daes Guards along the main road looking for

Gertrude. I have serious concerns that she didn't run away—she is uptight and has been set upon her duty as a princess her whole life. King Mason had always bragged about how *she knew her duty* and how that would make her a valuable queen for Charming. I just don't see her running away.

Charming is a whole other story. I met Cinderella after the wedding, and while I could see their genuine connection, I disapproved of the way Charming handled the situation. He knew that Father would never consent to break his betrothal to Princess Gertrude – and consequently the allegiance with the Kingdom of Daes – and snuck around manipulating everyone involved. He married her secretly, knowing that once he was married to her, there was nothing anyone could do. We had spoken about it at length while he was searching for her, and I tried to remind him of his commitments. The moment he saw Cinderella, then Gertrude, our Father, and his duties all vanished from his mind. He forgot about his arrangement to marry Gertrude and could only focus on finding his "Mystery Woman."

Arriving at our stables, I dismount and hand Onyx off to the stable manager. Usually, I would stay and care for him, taking the time to remove his saddle, brush his black coat and long mane, and feed him before I returned to my rooms. I don't have the time or patience for that today. I am still reeling that Gertrude is missing and that the Daes family think we have kidnapped her. Let alone everything that happened with Harrison. What type of monsters do they think we are? We'd had years of allegiance and friendship; do they not know us at all after all that time?

I storm through the castle towards my rooms, needing time to process everything that had happened before I discuss any of it with my family. I couldn't add more fuel to the fire that King Mason had already started. Luckily, I don't encounter anyone, and, closing myself inside, I sit down in my favourite brown leather armchair. I take out a journal and begin writing about everything that has happened today.

Writing in a journal has been a thinking process for me for

the last few years. I'd learnt that if I write it all down, it is easier for me to remove what's cluttering up my mind, and it is easier to think through the situation. Once I handled the situation, I tore the paper out of the journal and set it on fire, removing all trace of it from the world.

Taking a deep breath, I write down the words that Harrison burnt into my brain today. The self-doubt that rocked me earlier comes back with a vengeance, and I sift through those fears, breaking them down and analysing them. I had thought that I was convenient and he just no longer needed me; thought I pushed him to end things by being too demanding; thought that if I had been more, done more, we wouldn't be here. In my heart, I know that wasn't true.

But it doesn't change how he accused my family of kidnapping Gertrude. He cannot truly know me at all if he thinks I am capable of that.

For a moment, I allow myself to think that maybe the whole relationship was wrong. Perhaps our love was just confusion, miscommunication, and misunderstandings. Shaking myself out of my self-pity, I remind myself that he loves me. He just doesn't believe that he has a right to be happy if it causes unhappiness for others.

* * *

After taking the time to sort through and get in control of my emotions, I go in search of Charming. He has always been a close friend with Harrison; he might not know him as well as I do, but he may have an idea about what pressures Harrison is experiencing as an heir to the throne.

Charming is usually in his study at this time of the day. When I arrive, I am surprised to find it empty.

I hear a commotion at the other end of the hall. I walk to Father's study and knock on the door—perhaps Charming is in there with him, or at least Father might know where he is.

"Enter," Father's voice calls out. I let myself in. "Ah, Ambrose, glad you're joining us with everything that's going on."

"What's going on?"

"King Mason called upon Father this morning," Charming says. "He has accused us of kidnapping Princess Gertrude out of revenge. For what, I am unsure. We were the ones to break the arrangements; they would be the ones who should be vengeful."

"King Mason was here?" I ask.

"Yes, aren't you listening?" Charming huffs.

"He has declared us traitors to his kingdom," Father says solemnly.

"Well, more so than we already were," Charming interjects. "Gertrude is missing, and we are the only suspects in her disappearance, according to Father. King Mason believes that I have taken her as a mistress."

I force a shocked expression on my face to hide that I already know this. "We don't have her, do we?" I ask, needing to double-check.

"Of course not!" Father says.

"Why would we take such a sour and disagreeable person?" Charming says. "What would we have to gain from it? I never cared for Gertrude as she did me, and I don't want any mistresses. I am in love with and married to Cinderella, for fuck's sake. It would make more sense if they thought we stole her for you, but of course, we wouldn't do that."

"What are we doing then? Father, I am assuming you denied that we have her. Are we going to help them find her?"

"No!" Father says. "Why would we do that! They accused us of kidnapping."

"Maybe to prove that we didn't?" I offer.

"If we find her, it will only prove that we knew where she was and solidify their claim that we have her."

I understand what he is saying, but this is a woman's life we were discussing. She could be hurt or lost, or actually kidnapped by someone who would do horrible things to her.

"This isn't just anybody—this is Princess Gertrude," I say. "We've known her since we were children! If you're not going to do anything to help, then I will." No matter what Harrison said, I love him. His happiness is the most important thing in the world to me, and I know this situation is causing him distress.

"You can't go to them! They'll treat you like an enemy!" Charming snaps.

"I won't," I say, thinking out loud. "I'll find Princess Gertrude on my own, and I'll clear our name."

Father and Charming exchange a look I cannot decipher, and Father nods.

"Calm down, son," he says. "We'll do it together—we'll form our own search party, just not with them."

I release the breath I wasn't aware I was holding. At least we were going to do something to help find her.

"Okay, what do you need me to do?"

Chapter Four

HARRISON

Four years later

"What do you mean the guards haven't returned?" I demand of Joseph, who entered my study seconds ago.

"There have been no reports of the men since they entered the woods yesterday, Your Majesty," Joseph says, in a short and clipped manner.

"Any word or sighting of my sister?" I continue.

As Joseph opens his mouth to speak, Evalyn emerges from the open doorway, "Your sister, Your Majesty? Is that what all this fuss is over? Don't tell me you have actually found her?"

This is the last thing I want, and thankfully Joseph knows that.

"No, ma'am," Joseph replies, "Just a standard patrol. We had a prisoner who was a person of interest. We believed he might know of Princess Gertrude's whereabouts, but he has escaped in the night."

"I did not ask you, you fool. I asked the King." The fury at Joseph speaking for me evident in her voice, she turns back to me. "You suspect you can find her?"

"I don't know, Evalyn. What Joseph has just told you is the

truth. We currently do not know where she is; we haven't known for four years now."

I don't understand Gertrude, she had everything, and she ran away *twice*? She is a princess, had everything at her fingertips, and even had the chance to marry *him*, and she turns it all away for some backwoods man? I need to get to the bottom of this.

I stand up from my desk and walk over to look out the window over the palace garden and reflect on all that happened over the last four years. Ambrose's family burnt the Daes city of Adaira to the ground. Mother, Father, and King Kryler have died, and Charming and I have both ascended to the thrones of our respective Kingdoms.

Some good it's done me. My staff tries to keep it from me, but I know what the citizens whisper. The mad king. Insane and filled with rage.

I haven't seen or heard from Ambrose since the day that Evalyn found us in the garden here. There hasn't been a day in the last four years that I haven't thought about Ambrose or regretted what I said to him.

Every day I think about what I could have said or done differently. I yearn to reach out to him and have him back in my life. I don't know how to fix it or if there is even anything left to fix after everything I said to him. We almost wanted the same thing back then—who knew what Ambrose wanted now. Certainly not me—I pushed him away when the only thing I wanted to do was hold him closer.

In the first three days of Gertrude's disappearance, I had spoken strongly with my Father against Evalyn. I told him of her negligence in her duties and how she needed to be reprimanded or dismissed. He had dismissed other workers for far less than *misplacing* his daughter. I almost had Father convinced to get rid of her when she found me with Ambrose. Evalyn held that over my head and used it to have me persuade Father to let her stay on.

I remember the feeling of my gut twisting in shame and self-loathing at being manipulated by her. I have felt it every day since, and, along with the guilt I felt for Ambrose, it has been hard to focus on the rest of my life.

I quickly grew depressed after the events surrounding Gertrude's disappearance and my separation from Ambrose. Over the last four years, I have withdrawn from life in the palace and my court. I rarely go to any gatherings that were not essential, preferring to be alone than around people I don't like. Other's happiness takes mine away from me. Intentional or not, fair or not, I feel resentful. No one ever said feelings made sense.

Ambrose and Charming come to the forefront of my mind now. I didn't trust Ambrose when he told me there was no way that his family had Gertrude. Yet they burnt down Adaira. It doesn't make sense. When my father first approached King Kryler, they had a huge argument about it. I wasn't there. I didn't even know about the meeting until after it had taken place.

Father went a little mad after Gertrude disappeared. It was strange because, as Gertrude had said—yelled—at me in the throne room yesterday, mother and father didn't care about her when she was here. They left her for Evalyn to manage and only noticed her when it was of benefit to them, like the engagements to Charming, Ambrose, or Lord Damien.

To our parents, the pending announcement of her engagement to Charming completely eclipsed her actual eighteenth birthday. I remembered and ordered her a special lunch and dessert for dinner. She never knew that it was me. I also ordered her a new book written by one of her favourite authors, but it did not arrive until the spring when she was already gone. I still have it wrapped up on the bookcase in my room, waiting for her return.

I was a fool. I shouldn't have thrown Gertrude in the cells. I let my anger at Father, at Evalyn, and at myself get in the way, but I knew in my soul she wasn't a criminal or a spy. I allowed myself to be manipulated for far too long now, allowing doubt to wriggle into my mind and affect the way I acted and thought.

"I am such a fucking idiot," I mutter under my breath to myself.

Not for one moment did I show any joy or excitement that she had made her way home after four years. No wonder she ran away again—she probably thought I was going to kill her or keep her locked up forever. My actions would not have done much to convince her otherwise. I have spent my life trying to make everyone else happy, but I ended up miserable and hurting the people that truly matter to me.

Now, she is probably assuming the worst, wherever she has gone. The moment the guards realised that her cell was empty last night, Joseph sent out a patrol to locate her and bring her safely back home. We had never had someone escape from those cells before, and both Joseph and I were shocked to discover the hinges removed from their cell doors.

I grew up learning to follow the rules and traditions—to stick with the procedures that had been laid out for centuries, and to stay faithful to the oaths and vows I swore at my coronation. In addition, to other standards to which I held myself—the most important being to admit when I was wrong or made a mistake, and to fix the situation.

Admitting to myself that it was wrong to imprison Gertrude is relatively easy, but I don't know how I can fix the situation, nor the one that Father made with King Kryler and King Charming.

A throat clears and brings me out of my introspection. Blinking a few times, I turn to find that Evalyn and Joseph are still in the room with me.

"Why are you still here, Evalyn?" It sounded like I meant the room, but I also thought about the kingdom in general. Since I convinced my father to reinstate her position in the household, she has been a thorn in my side. Lingering and lording herself over me, over my kingdom, holding my world in the balance. I ascended to the throne and allowed her to stay. She was in a position of power as an advisor—as a Lady of the court. She managed liaisons with other lands, Ladies and Lords.

"I came to see you, Your Majesty. I heard about the escaped prisoner and thought I could be of assistance and help you to *release* some stress." She replies in what I am sure she thinks is a sexy voice, which only grates on my nerves and annoys me.

"And how exactly are you going to help? Are you going to go out on horseback and look for them?" She glares at my sarcasm. "I need to speak with Joseph alone, Evalyn. Can you please leave now?"

She huffs and turns, sashaying out of the room. The events of the last twenty-four hours have set off several epiphanies. I realise I have had enough of her and her attitude. In the last few years, I had grown accustomed to her presence, engaging with her as little as possible, ignoring her attempted advances, and allowing her to control my kingdom through me. With my struggle with depression and lack of interest, it was easier to permit her to do as she pleased, rather than draw up the energy to challenge her.

I need her out of my life and my kingdom. I don't know how I can accomplish that yet. I look at Joseph, who doesn't conceal his hatred of Evalyn.

"Now that she is gone, what do we need to discuss, Your Majesty?"

"Gertrude and Ika. They are not prisoners on the run. I do not want them treated as such. She is a princess and my sister; I was wrong for locking her up. I would like it conveyed if they are found, they are not to be harmed." Joseph's shoulders visibly relax, grateful, and agreeing with what I was saying. I continue, "Send more guards out into the forest, have them look for the other guards, and I will also give them a letter for Gertrude if they happen to find her. I want her safe and home. We also need to reach out to King Charming. I will write a letter now that is to be delivered urgently."

"Of course, Your Majesty. I will go and organise the parties now. When would you like me to return for the letters?"

"Give me half an hour."

Joseph bows in acceptance and leaves the room. I return to my desk and write letters to King Charming, to Ambrose, and several copies of a message for Gertrude.

King Charming,

I hope this letter finds you well. I am reaching out in the wishes of mending alliances and hopefully ending the feud between us.

This animosity was caused by our fathers, who never thought about the consequences of their actions and are not here to see things through. As we have not attacked each other since their respective deaths, I think it is safe to assume you would be open to a resolution.

Firstly, I would like to apologise for the actions of my father that started this situation. I knew from the beginning that you wouldn't have taken Gertrude, but I lost myself under the stress and anxiety of a missing sister and became vulnerable to the suggestions of those around me. For a while, I believed my father, believed that he knew the only logical solution to where Gertrude was. I don't say this to antagonise you; I am just hoping you can understand what I have mentally and emotionally been going through over the last four years.

I have news on this front that I would like to share with you but would prefer it if we continued this conversation in person. Please

grant me the time to meet with you to discuss these matters further that will hopefully allow us to come to an agreement that is mutually beneficial for both our kingdoms.
Regards,
King Harrison

grant me the time to meet with you to discuss these matters further that will hopefully allow us to come to an agreement that is mutually beneficial for both our kingdoms.

Chapter Five

AMBROSE

It has been years, but I haven't given up hope, not yet.

I have spent every waking moment looking for leads, investigating locations, and scouring the Jang Forest in hopes of finding Gertrude. Riding back through the burnt remains of Adaira now reminds me of when Gertrude first went missing. Eager to help in any way I could, I had travelled the road between our kingdoms in the hope that someone had any idea where Gertrude could have gone.

On that first day searching, I was pleasantly surprised in Adaira to find out that a woman matching her description had been in town the same day she had gone missing. I had practically interrogated the stable hand and the village president's daughter, Rosemary, who were the only people to have spoken with the stranger that had visited them. Rosemary told me everything she could remember about the visitor, explaining the tour and the conversations they had. The visitor went by the name of "Trudy Knight," and it was too close a name and description for me to believe it was anyone other than Gertrude Daes.

"She was meant to return three days later, to speak with my father about artists' contact details and how she could get artworks commissioned. Prince Charming had just purchased all the work in our galleries, you see, and Trudy was very upset that she was not able to purchase any of the work for her collection," I remember Rosemary saying to me. It was definitely Princess Gertrude.

"When she left, do you know where she went?"

Rosemary showed me the path that Trudy left on, and I knew there was a fork in the road. One way led to her palace, the other further into the woods. It was a lead, and I had no time to waste. I sent an urgent message to my father, telling him what I learned. I headed off down the path and into the woods, looking for any traces of Gertrude. Finding nothing and out of supplies, I returned to the small inn I was staying at in Adaira. I was there the night my father burned it down.

I woke up to pounding on my door and one of my father's guards telling me that I had to leave. I ran to my father and tried to stop him. I had to watch as my father's men boarded up the rest of the village and burned it to the ground. His men had to restrain me as I kept fighting, trying to save someone, anyone, from the destruction that my father was causing.

I often wondered what King Mason and Harry thought about that night. Father had made a statement burning that village—saying that Gertrude had been there and now Harry and King Mason wouldn't know where to look for her. I was ashamed and disgusted.

I lost faith in my father, and I no longer wanted anything to do with him or what he stood for. I distanced myself from Charming too—not once had he tried to convince Father not to attack Adaira, nor did he help with finding Gertrude. They had outright lied to me—they were not interested in helping her or returning her home. They just wanted to increase the amount of pain that King Mason and the Daes family had to endure. And for what? Heated words said during a moment of stress and trouble?

King Mason hadn't been a saint, and he was known to have a

temper. His conversations with Father probably could have been handled better, but his daughter was missing! I would assume anyone wouldn't be thinking correctly in that situation.

With Adaira destroyed, I returned to living in the castle and camping in the woods for one or two nights at a time. I did not stop looking for Gertrude, but now I didn't tell Charming anything I knew.

I have a small group of friends that I spend time with when I am home. A few men in the court that I know can be trusted and know what I am really looking for in the woods. Charming had long since given up on caring what I did when I left the Castle, often telling people I was just off on "another quest."

I told myself I needed to find Gertrude for mine and Harrison's peace of mind. I haven't seen him since our argument. It hurt to have him not trust me or believe me. Still, after time reflecting and having emotionally distanced myself from the past, I realised his reaction had more to do with his emotional state than my family or me.

I haven't been with anyone else over the last four years. Harrison is my one and only, and I have not been able to move on. He didn't want to be public, and I didn't want to hide—not that I have come out in the four years that have passed, not even Charming knows that I am gay—I don't see how we could have stayed together without hurting each other, but I never stopped loving him. Maybe once I see him married or found Gertrude, I would be able to accept his decision and move on.

Another week with no results. I had scoured the woods for years looking for any trace. As hard as it is to admit to myself, I am beginning to lose hope of ever finding her.

* * *

I return to the castle to find everything as I left it the week earlier. Charming and Cinderella are happily lost in their little world and don't notice my return. Cinderella is pregnant and expecting their first child, and she is due to give birth any day now. I thought they would have had kids earlier; they have been married for four years now. Charming once told me he wanted to give them time to solidify their love alone together and to allow Cinderella time to enjoy being free of responsibilities. I know very little about her life before meeting Charming and her upbringing outside of the basic information. Cinderella isn't ashamed of her past—however, I know it causes her and Charming pain to remember the horrors of her life before meeting Charming.

Returning to my rooms, I begin undressing for a much-needed bath when there is a knock at my door.

"Enter," I call out, putting my shirt on the counter. Standing there shirtless, I look up to see a maid has entered with a letter in her hand. Her eyes land on my naked chest, and she freezes, staring, her eyes raking up and down my chest and abs as she licks her lips.

"What's that?" I ask bluntly, drawing her out of her daze. I don't have the patience today to deal with women trying to bed me. I am too exhausted after another trying week with no outcome.

"A-a-a Letter from King Harrison, Your Highness," she stutters out.

I nearly choke on my breath, barely managing to pass it off as clearing my throat. "Leave it on the dresser; you can go."

Getting braver, she takes a step towards me and brazenly asks, "Do you need anything, Your Highness?"

"No. Leave," I growl out. When will the women who work here get the hint that I don't want to sleep with them? You would think they would get the idea after twenty-two fucking years. I wait as she scrambles from the room before I look at the letter she placed on the dresser, afraid that she will see my reaction to hearing from him.

I haven't spoken to him in four years, and anticipation and fear spike through me. Too anxious to wait and puzzle over what could be inside the letter, I break the wax seal and try not to rip the letter in my haste to get it open. With trembling hands, I hold the letter as I read and re-read the words written out in Harrison's neat handwriting. I've kept some of the old letters from our previous lives —the ones that weren't too incriminating —written to me in his tidy script. I destroyed the others. I hadn't realised how much I had missed receiving letters from him until I was holding a new one in my hand. Each stroke of ink cuts through me, tearing open the wounds on my heart yet giving me a flicker of hope that he could help me heal too.

My dearest Ro,
There are so many things I need to say to you. I know you probably don't want to hear from me after everything that happened between us four years ago and between our families in the years since. I would under-stand if you hate me. Bearing all this in mind, I hope you grant me the time it will take for you to read this letter. It might not change anything, and yet, there are some things I need you to know.
Firstly, I am sorry. I am so sorry about the things I said to you in the garden. You didn't deserve my words or my lack of trust. I should have told you long before now, I have been a coward using grief and excuses to prevent myself from reaching out to you.
The moment the words came out of my mouth, I knew that it was wrong to say them to you and even to consider them at all. You have always been trustworthy, honest, and open with me. You never lied or gave me a reason to believe that you would be dishonest. I wish I could

claim I never doubted you; unfortunately, I allowed the ideas and judgements of others to worm their way into my mind and take up camp. I am sorry I allowed them to influence my thoughts about you.

For the longest time, I have let my self-worth be dictated to me, based on other people's opinions and remarks. I know that you are aware of some of it, but there were parts that I didn't even tell you. It is why I said no to you all those years ago. I'm sorry if this is bringing everything you don't want to hear back to the surface, but I love you—I never stopped loving you. I have loved you since I was sixteen, and it still pains me that I hurt you. I wish there were something I could do to enable us to have the future we both wanted then. That I still want now.

Secondly, Gertrude was found. She made her way home and returned yesterday morning. Clearly, I haven't stopped being an idiot in the last four years, as I locked her in a cell. I was so caught up in my father's slander that I had truly believed she was held captive in your kingdom by Charming. I actually said to her face that Charming must have gotten bored of his whore—I also accused her of being turned into a spy. It took her escaping from the cell and the palace for me to remember that she is still the sister that I have always loved and missed.

She was trapped in the Silent Wood of all places, still within our kingdom. She didn't even realise that four fucking years had passed. She showed up thinking it had only been a day. She had stumbled her way out of the forest and to this Ika fellow's house. He brought her home to me. She escaped later that night with him, and we haven't been able to find them since. I sent guards into the Jang Forest when her escape was reported to me. They have gone missing. I know she is running away because she thinks I'll hurt or punish them — but I only want her safe and at home. I was an idiot for imprisoning her, and now I have lost her again. With no way to contact her, I am worried about her safety and also her getting into a bad situation in attempts to escape me.

I have also sent a letter to your brother in the hope of ending the strain and animosity between our kingdoms. Our fathers set this in motion and are not here to see it through. I hope that someday soon, we may be able to build new bridges between our kingdoms.

I'm sure you remember Evalyn finding us that day in the garden. She hasn't told anyone about what she saw, but it came at a cost to me. She has been living here and been a part of my court for the last four years. Evalyn finds a way to manipulate every decision and order I make, using her information about us against me. I have started searching for a way out of her grip, but I don't know what contingencies she has in place.

Enough about that, though. Evalyn isn't the reason I am writing to you. I wanted you to know that I am sorry and have been for the

last four years, and that Gertrude was safe
before I fucked that up again.
I assume you have moved on, as you should
have. I hate that we still live in a world
where I cannot see a way we could be
together. If you are still reading at this
point, I would also like to thank you. Thank
you for always being my best friend and the
most wonderful man that I have ever known. I
wish I could go back and change what I said,
to be brave enough to claim you as I wanted
to. I wish we were able to be together,
openly, and rule together. It is my sincerest
wish. I hope that someday soon, I will be
able to see your smiling face, and that you
will be able to forgive me for the foolish
and idiotic things I have done.
Eternally Yours,
Harry.

I read over the words again, absorbing all the information. Gertrude was found but is now missing again. Reading about Harry locking Gertrude up was hard. It hurts me to think about the type of man that Harry has become if he thought that it was a good idea.

The Silent Wood stretches throughout the Jang Forest within the Kingdom of Daes. I didn't put much stock in it for a long time, believing it was all a myth. In my search for Gertrude, I came across many stories and accounts of the Silent Wood and had found the rough border of the enchanted area. Often, it's hard to tell when someone goes missing within the Silent Wood, as they are never seen again. It makes it impossible to confirm what has happened to them. I'd never looked too close in there as I wasn't sure how much of the stories were true. For Gertrude to have been lost there, and then find her way home, is a fantastic feat in itself.

The other part of his letter that stands out to me is the name Ika. I know him. He is a lumberjack living in the Jang Forest. I don't know where exactly, other than somewhere backing onto the border between the two kingdoms. I remember him from the aftermath of the fire of Adaira—he arrived later and tried to stop the fire as I did. Most importantly, I now know where to start looking for Gertrude.

Chapter Six

HARRISON

I didn't have to wait long for a response to my letter to King Charming. Early in the afternoon, our messenger returned with a letter, asking me to meet him at twilight in Adaira. I rushed to get organised and arrive on time.

Now, standing in the village centre waiting for Charming to arrive, needing a distraction, I look at the destruction around me. Where buildings once stood, only charred bricks remain. The forest was regrowing and encroaching on the once burnt land. I pace as my mind races, thinking back to my past decisions and my time with Ambrose.

Memories assault me; the first time I made him blush, our first kiss, our argument at Charming's ball, and when we finally said we love each other.

Had I been selfish, allowing us to fall into a relationship when I knew nothing could come of it? Had it been true love from the beginning, or was I just a horny teenager, more interested in getting off without care for the consequences?

Looking back, I cannot say if I initially pursued Ambrose from love, boredom, or lust. Whatever way that I fell into the relationship is no longer relevant; the result is the same. I fell in love with him, *and inevitably ruined it*, I remind myself. I hurt the man that means the world to me, and for what? A throne, the happiness of my court, and my citizens. I had been so focused on being a future king and appeasing everyone else that I could only see the future that had been dictated to me. Standing here now, it's suddenly not enough.

A new resolve fills me. I have to accept myself and be okay with who I am. I cannot dwell on the past any longer. I can't change it, can't fix what I did. But I can change what my priorities are. I hadn't admitted that I am gay to anyone other than Ambrose and Joseph. How can I expect to run a kingdom if I can't even be honest with myself?

A snapping branch brings me out of my thoughts. I look up to see Charming approaching, three guards flanking him. I am glad that I also did not bring excess protection as Joseph had wanted me to do so. I had my usual two guards and Joseph behind me, and I could hear them move into a protective circle as Charming's group approaches.

Charming looks the same as I remember—pale and stick-thin with cropped black hair—the same hair as his brother. His face brings back fond memories, and a smile tugs at the corner of my mouth. It turns into a frown as I notice that Ambrose isn't here, even though I knew he probably wouldn't be.

"King Charming, thank you for meeting with me today." We were never formal as children; however, I am unsure how he would take it if I addressed him informally now.

"King Harrison, good to see you again," he replies, extending his hand for me to shake. Grasping his hand, I relax and smile slightly at him.

"Good to see you too. How is everything going for you?"

"Good, good. I read your letter, and the only reason I am here today is because of Cinderella's urging. I think there has been enough said between our kingdoms and would have left well enough alone, but she convinced me to hear you out and settle everything, if only for our child's sake."

"You have a child?" This is news to me. The information

between kingdoms was limited since King Kryler began monitoring the citizens who crossed the border. Charming had ceased this after his death, but people are still cautious and limit their travel.

"We are expecting; the baby is due any day now, so you will understand I cannot stay long."

"Of course! If I had known, I would have been happy to meet you at your castle to prevent your travel." But he had been the one to suggest Adaira—he must have wanted me away from Cinderella in case I had been planning a trap. I can respect him for being so careful.

"In your letter, you said you wanted to make amends and had news about Princess Gertrude." He states. No more small talk then, it seems.

"Yes. I believe we have both had a hand in events over the years that we aren't proud of. This dispute began with our fathers and has settled somewhat since they both passed. Both sides have acted in anger and defence, and I think it's time we resolve this. Additionally, Gertrude returned home the day before yesterday. The whole situation is in shambles, but she confirmed she was trapped in the Silent Wood, and she didn't realise she had been missing for four years."

"So, you are only apologising now that she has returned?"

"I am sorry; it took her returning to wake me up from my delusions. If I could go back and change things and prevent this whole situation from happening, I would. However, I don't think your family has been blameless in this either. You started the initial feud by marrying Cinderella. I don't fault you for that, particularly; however, it was poorly executed. I haven't seen you together to confirm it myself, but I received reports that you are incredibly happy, and that's more than our parents could say for their marriages. You also burnt Adaira to the ground to send a message. I think we both have things to apologize for."

"It was Father who burnt the village," Charming replies, looking troubled by the memory he glances to where the Art

Galleries once stood—stone walls now half crumbled to the ground, covered in moss and vines. "Ambrose and I began helping look for Gertrude, believing Father was trying to help. He had told us that he was trying to find her and would keep her safe until your father 'came to his senses.' The moment Father betrayed us and burnt Adaira, it broke us. He actually went behind my back to do it. Ambrose was staying in the village at the time and only managed to escape because of Gavin here," he points at one of the guards behind him, who was tall and wide with cropped short blonde hair and pale blue eyes. "He knew where he was and woke him up before he could be trapped."

My gut sours, why would Gavin know where Ambrose was staying if he wasn't *with* him? I took a deep breath and made an effort to control my features preventing Charming, Gavin, and the others from seeing my rioting emotions. I had known Ambrose would move on eventually—I just hadn't expected it to be so soon after our split. Especially as I haven't moved on, I have not been with anyone other than Ambrose. Adaira was lost over three years ago, so clearly, Ambrose had moved on pretty quickly. *You have no right to be jealous. You left him, remember?*

"We didn't speak with him after that, not until he was on his deathbed," Charming goes on. "Even then, the bastard didn't apologise. He claimed it was his right, his duty to cause you and your father pain and put you in your place."

"By the way, where is Ambrose?" I mentally slap myself the moment the words escape.

"He returned this morning but left again in a hurry this afternoon. You know how he has always been, off on quests and adventures. He is rarely home for more than a day or two at a time these days."

"Ah, okay then," I mumble, not very intelligently.

"What are you proposing, Harrison? You haven't exactly said how we should move forward."

"I propose we forgive, forget, and move on. We both agree that our fathers made errors. We aren't our fathers, and we don't need to continue their meaningless conflicts for them. I propose we negotiate new alliances and trade agreements, and I would be happy to arrange a future meeting to have that conversation. Right now, I suppose I am looking for an agreement that this feud is over, and if we can't go back to being friends, to at least be acquaintances."

Charming glances at the men around us. "Would you all give us a moment alone? Step back thirty paces, so we are still visible, but ensure you can no longer hear our conversation."

Charming's men follow the order immediately, whereas Joseph looks to me for confirmation. I nod, and they retreat, turning to watch us again. Charming remains silent, waiting until all the men were out of hearing range.

"What of Ambrose, Harry?" He asks in a quiet voice, further ensuring that we would not be overheard.

"What do you mean?" I reply, equally quiet. Fear quickly jolts through me. Did Ambrose tell him?

"Don't treat me like an idiot; we both know I'm not one. I know you and Ambrose were together before the ball, where this all started. He is my little brother, and I know him almost as well as I know myself. I knew from when we were about seventeen that there was something between the two of you, although he never told me. Honestly, it's the only reason that I allowed your mother to pair me off with your sister all the time so that you two could have some time together."

He... What...?

"I need to know," Charming continues, "Is this all an attempt to get him back? I watched him in the months between my twenty-first birthday and Gertrude's disappearance; I saw how depressed he was—is, and I know it is related to you. He tried to hide it, but I can see through his façade. I'm not blind. What are you hoping to achieve?"

"If he hasn't told you, I don't want to break his confidence. Although, I can't see a future where we are together. This meeting is about our kingdoms, not my relationships."

"Surely, it could not have been so bad that you can't forgive each other?"

"It's not only forgiveness that I need." My eyes flick back to Gavin. "I think he has moved on, and he should have. I didn't see how we could be together then or now. How can we when I am King? Besides—"

Charming's laughter cuts me off, "You are a King, Harrison! Last time I checked, they do whatever they wanted and fucked off anyone who disagreed with them. Take that leaf out of our fathers' book if nothing else: Do what you want and what will make you happy. Everyone else can either fall in line or leave."

"Well, when you put it that way..." I reply sheepishly. Charming explaining it like that makes me feel like an even bigger idiot.

"I'll speak to him when he gets home, okay? I'll tell him about Gertrude and our new alliance. Maybe he will come and speak to you after that."

I squash down the hope that blooms in my chest. If he was home this morning, he should have received my letter. His absence means I can only assume he doesn't want anything to do with me. Either he didn't read the letter, or he did, and it means nothing to him.

"You'll agree to an alliance then?" I hedge, trying to change the subject smoothly, but I can see in his eyes that he knows. Thankfully, he allows it.

"Yes, Harrison," he replies, "we were always good friends growing up, and I hope that we can get back to that. I will issue a notice to my citizens informing them of our agreement. I have to get back to Cindy now, but I will write to you to arrange a meeting at my castle within the next fortnight. I don't want to travel far so soon after the birth."

"Of course, I understand. I will be happy to come to you."

We shake hands again before turning and walking towards our guards. It feels good to have put everything to rest, and a weight I didn't realise I was carrying on my shoulders lifts.

Whatever may come from the situation with Ambrose, I have new options to consider. I have to accept myself for who I am. Maybe I am not worthy of Ambrose, but I am worthy of love.

I am a King, and I can do what I want. I can be openly gay. I can love a man, marry a man. I just need to be brave enough to do it.

Chapter Seven

AMBROSE

Usually, when I return to the castle after a week away, I stay for two or three days, spending time enjoying the company of friends, reviewing any notes and maps, and giving Onyx a break. With this new information on Gertrude, I cannot wait – I have to go now. Without taking the time to say goodbye to anyone, I quickly gather supplies and saddle Onyx back up, heading out of our kingdom, towards Adaira and the Kingdom of Daes.

Our castle is on the eastern edge of our kingdom and is only an hour's ride from Adaira. I have a rough estimation of where the Silent Wood starts and veers south, slowing down as I cross the border into the Daes Kingdom. My reports say the best way to tell where the Silent Wood starts is to watch the wildlife and listen for noises. If the stories I've collected and the rough map I created with my research are correct, I should be close to the Silent Wood now.

I slow Onyx to a trot and listen to the forest around us. The silence of the forest on my left is intense. I think I am on the edge of the Silent Wood. I am amazed that it is real. Harry is going to be so shocked when he learns I believe in the Silent Wood.

Harry.

A sigh escapes me, causing me to slap myself mentally. I cannot daydream and risk ending up in the Silent Wood myself. Focusing again on my surroundings, I lead Onyx through the forest, ensuring that I keep the silence on my left side and making our path through the trees.

The sun is high in the sky now, and it is creeping into the early hours of the afternoon. I have been walking next to the Silent Wood for an hour now. As I think about taking a break, a flickering light ahead catches my eye. I dismount Onyx and tie him up. He is well trained and usually, I would leave him to graze, knowing he wouldn't wander far, but being this close to the Silent Wood has me taking this extra precaution. Slowly, I walk closer to the glittering light, being careful to conceal my footsteps and tread carefully over fallen branches and twisted roots. Once I am a few metres away, I can make out it is a wind chime. It is made out of polished metal and wood, hanging from a large old pine tree.

It is an odd place to hold such detailed work, and I approach to investigate it further. The bark was cleared behind the charm, and there is a sunflower etched into the wood with the words:

Free is the spirit of Tomeka and her Fredrick,
Vast is the joy and love they share.
No longer made of blood and bone,
Their days of pain and suffering are gone.
They live on within the soul of their son,
Shining and singing his way home when the day is done.

It is beautiful and heart-warming. I don't know who Tomeka and Fredrick were, yet considering this tribute's location, I assume they are somehow connected to Ika. I don't know of anyone else living in this area of the forest, and hopefully, this was a sign I am getting close to Ika's home.

I remount Onyx, anticipation coursing through my veins at the thought of being so close to finding Gertrude after all these years. We continue further into the wood, taking care to walk around the memorial tree out of respect for Tomeka and Fredrick. About a hundred metres past the wind chime, a clearing comes into view, and I almost yell out in relief. There, in front of a large empty field, is a cabin, a large barn, and a paddock area holding Gertrude's horse, Stormy.

I found Ika's home, found Gertrude! Momentarily overwhelmed with relief, I sit and stare at the cabin. I did it.

Maintaining a steady walking pace, I guide Onyx around to the front of the cabin. They must be on edge after escaping imprisonment, and I don't want to startle them. Dismounting, I leave Onyx to linger and walk up the steps of the cabin. I raise my hand to knock on the door and hesitate when I see my hand is shaking. Hand still hovering in the air, the door swings open. Ika stands there, the same stoic expression on his face that he wore the last time I saw him.

"How can I help you?" he clips out in a barely civil tone.

"I'm looking for Princess Gertrude." Anger bleeds across his face, and before I see it coming, his fist shoots out and punches me square in the face. I hear the crunch of my nose and feel the blood pour down my face before I fall to my knees, and the world goes black.

Chapter Eight

TRUDY

Shocked did not even begin to cover the emotions racing through me. When we heard steps on the porch, Ika clicked into protection mode instantly. He pushed me into his bedroom before stomping to the front door.

"I am looking for Princess Gertrude," a deep rumbling voice replied and was followed by a crunching noise, then something thudding to the floor.

Concern for Ika overcoming any sense of self-protection, I run out to the front door to find Ika looking down at a man. He is tan and muscular, has wavy black hair, and is flat on his back, unconscious. Blood is running all over his swelling face.

"...Ambrose?" My eyes flicker over his face and up to Ika.

From the look of Ika's left hand, he punched Ambrose in the face and broke his nose.

"What happened?"

"He was looking for you. Now we have time to figure out what he is after."

I'm still trying to comprehend that Ambrose is here at Ika's —no, our—home. Ika hoists Ambrose up into his arms and carries him into the house.

"Pass me the reins by the door, Darlin'." He says while setting

Ambrose down in one of the wooden chairs. Without questioning it, I retrieve the reins for Ika, as I have absolute trust in him. He uses them to tie Ambrose's arms and legs to the chair.

"It won't hold him long—Ambrose is a knight, Ika. He will know how to get out of a simple binding."

"I know Darlin', but it's enough for now."

I rush to the kitchen cupboard and pull out an old tattered wash rag and a bowl of water.

"What are you doing, Darlin'?" he says with amusement in his voice. I look over my shoulder at him. His small smile and quirked eyebrow knock the breath out of me. How could I be so lucky to find this man?

"You broke his nose, and there is blood everywhere," I push the bowl of water and rag into Ika's hands, "and you can clean it up. I'm not having any more blood in my home."

Ika's eyes shimmer and seem brighter as he stares down at me. Have I pissed him off?

"Say it again," Ika's voice is low and husky. My skin breaks out in goose bumps as a shiver runs down my spine.

"Wh-what?" He is confusing me. "Why are you suddenly so intense?"

"The part where you called it your home." He says, ignoring my question.

"Are you angry?" I ask tentatively.

"Angry?" he blinks several times, taking a moment to rethink the situation. His gaze softens as he continues, "No, Darlin, I ain't angry. Why would I be? It is one of the sexiest things to ever come out of your mouth."

Oh. "Oh!"

Ika chuckles, leaning forward, he captures my lips in a searing kiss. Just like every kiss with Ika, I am captivated by him. I lose track of time and myself—there is nothing and no one around but the two of us; I feel only his body against mine and the emotions swirling between us. The sexual tension between us had been building since our night in the forest.

We had only gotten here yesterday and were too exhausted to do anything other than wash and rest. Thankfully, he still had a portion of his mother's wardrobe, and we were the same size, so I was able to have clean clothing. I think Ika liked me having something of his mother's. I wish I had known her and his father.

Each small touch and kiss grow the anticipation inside of me. I had been too nervous to broach the subject today, self-conscious about how to start that conversation. The heat and passion in this kiss tell me that the conversation might not need to be with words. His hands still hold the bowl and rag, but my hands had snuck up into his long luscious hair.

A groan from Ambrose brings us back to the present, and we hastily pull away from each other. Ika's eyes are full of heat and desire, telling me that this isn't over. Ambrose isn't awake yet, but he is starting to stir. With ease and precision, Ika cleans most of the blood from Ambrose's face and chest before cleaning up the drops of blood that made their way onto the floorboards.

Sitting down, I use the table as an extra barrier between me and Ambrose, for protection, as well as space to absorb everything that is going on. I turn and made eye contact with Ika, who is returning from the kitchen after emptying the bowl.

"Why is he looking for me?" I ask. I know that Ika won't be able to answer, but I need to say it anyway. "How did he know where to find us? If everything you and Harrison said is true, and we have been in a feud with King Charming and Prince Ambrose, then why is he looking for us?"

"Several reasons, Princess Gertrude. Will you give me the chance to explain them, or will punchy over there interrupt me again?" Ambrose grunts out, alerting us to his consciousness. His voice is nasally and affected by his broken nose.

Holding in my laughter at "punchy," I turn to Ambrose. "Speak, but if you don't get to the point soon, I will not prevent any more punches. Start with how you found me."

"I knew Ika lived in this area of the woods, and I knew you were with him in the palace and left with him, so I started looking in the area late this morning."

"Why?"

"Harry told me that you returned and ran away again. He told me about how you were trapped in the Silent Wood and found Ika and your way home. He also told me how he reacted badly and wanted to find you to reassure you that he was an idiot."

"Why would he tell you? A few days ago, all he had to say was that our kingdoms weren't speaking with each other due to everything that happened while I was missing."

"There's a lot you don't know, Gertrude, and I am not sure if Harrison would want me to tell you all of it."

"Don't talk down to her," Ika growls out, stepping up behind me and resting his hand on my shoulder. Thankfully, it was his right hand, which wasn't bruising due to punches. At his touch, a jolt of fire courses through my skin. This is not the time! I berate myself.

"You'd better start explaining, Ambrose, and don't leave anything out. Are you here to capture us and take us back to Harrison? What does he want? Can't he just be happy that I am no longer his problem?"

"He never saw you as a problem, Gertrude. Harrison has always had trouble fighting with appearances, against what he wants, and what others around him want of him. It will be easier for him to explain it himself, that's why I came here to take you home to him. He won't hurt you or lock you up again."

"This is my home now. I don't want to go back to that prison—"

Ambrose cuts me off, his eyebrows lifting in surprise before scrunching in confusion, "He won't lock you up again, I can guarantee that."

I clench my jaw so tight I thought my teeth were going to break.

"The palace was her prison, Ambrose," Ika answers for me in his soft, smooth voice. His hand squeezes my shoulder in comfort. His touch soothes me, and I feel the tension drain out of me.

"Would you let him come here?" Ambrose suddenly asks, "I think it's something he needs to do, speaking to you in person. You might need it, too, to be able to resolve the unease between you. You were always one of his highest priorities."

"His priority?" I scoff. "You didn't see the way he treated me when we weren't at functions."

"No, I didn't. But I knew what he felt and thought."

"How? I know you were friends, but I doubt even the two of you were that close."

"Harry is going to hate me for this, but you need to know. It's the only way that this will move forward."

"Know what?" Ika asks. Sudden gratefulness for Ika slams into me. Not once has he tried to control me—he has stayed and supported me, but he doesn't try and take over or cut me out like my parents, Evalyn, and occasionally even Harrison, had done all my life.

I looked up at Ika over my shoulder and met his gaze.

"I love you," I tell him, my voice calm and controlled. Saying those words are the most natural thing I have ever said. He is the only person I have ever said those words to; not even my family had heard me say them. I watch the emotions play over his face, leaning down Ika cups my face, injured hand and all.

"I love you, Darlin'." He breathes against my lips, claiming my mouth with a kiss. I had never kissed anyone before Ika, so I had nothing to compare it to, but every kiss with Ika was an experience in itself. My hands curl against his chest, twisting into his shirt and pulling him closer to me. One of his hands remains to cup my face while the other twists around my skull and into my hair, fisting it and pulling it slightly, angling my head to deepen our kiss.

"I'm glad you guys love each other," Ambrose interjects, with a tinge of sarcasm, "but remember you aren't alone before anything goes too far." I pull back from Ika. He was right—I had forgotten.

"I'm sorry," I utter, trying to compose myself. Turning in my seat to face Ambrose again, I feel my face and chest flush hot with a blush.

"I'm not," Ika growls in my ear, nipping at the lobe lightly before straightening.

"Right, well," I clear my throat, "What do we need to know?"

"I don't want to break Harrison's confidence with strangers. I can tell you, Gertrude, but I can't tell Ika."

"Either you tell us both, or you don't tell either of us. It's that simple. Ika is my, my..." I try to think of a word that can cover precisely what Ika is to me. Our relationship isn't something established or labelled so far. It's only a few days old, and yet it is eternal. "Everything," I say breathily, "He is my everything. I trust him completely, therefore you can tell us both."

Ambrose sighs, watching me as he thinks over my offer.

"I can't hurt Harrison like that. He hasn't told you for a reason. However, I suppose you can read a letter he wrote to me and come to your own conclusions..." He trails off.

"Do you have a letter on you?"

"There is one in the left breast pocket of my jacket if one of you would like to withdraw it." He replies, tugging at his restraints to indicate he is unable to withdraw it himself.

Ika walks around the table to Ambrose's side and reaches into his jacket pocket, withdrawing an envelope. Returning to my side, Ika hands me the letter and places his hand on my shoulder again, reading along over my shoulder.

I read the first line of the letter and can tell instantly it is Harrison's handwriting. Once, twice, a third time, I read through his words, checking to make sure I understand it correctly. Each time the same sentences stuck out to me:

...*For the longest time, I have let my self-*

worth be dictated to me, based on other people's opinions and remarks…

…I have always loved you…

…I was an idiot for accusing her, and now I have lost her again…

…Evalyn finds a way to manipulate every decision and order I have, using her information about us against me…

…I wish we were able to be together, openly, and rule together; it is my deepest wish…

"You were together?" I ask him.

Ambrose's only response is a single nod.

"You came here because of Harrison?" I ask, and Ambrose's face contorts like he is mentally at war with what he should say.

Taking a deep breath, he says, "Gertrude, I never stopped looking for you. Every day for the last four years, the only thing I could think about or do was to find you. Find you for Harrison. And as a way to distract myself from my heartache. You should have seen him when you went missing. It was Harrison who noticed you weren't at the palace—he had to convince everyone that you had gone. He was so distraught he believed that you really had been kidnapped by my father or Charming. There were some awful words exchanged between us that day."

Ambrose's eyes grow distant, trapped inside the memory of that day. I glance up at Ika, smiling reassuringly at me, and peace settles in me. I offer him a tentative smile, turning back to Ambrose. No matter what happens now, I have Ika to help me.

Ambrose shakes his head, and his eyes refocus on the present. "Do you get it now? Do you understand why I had to come here and take you to him? If Ika is your everything, then Harrison is mine."

"How long has this been going on?" I ask, curiosity bubbling within me.

"We first kissed when I was fourteen, and he was seventeen."

"That long? How did I not know?"

"No one knew—that was one of our issues. And that is a story for another time. Will you please untie me so we can go to him?"

"No!" All friendly feelings in me dry up. "I am not going back there. I believe you are genuine in your attempts to help my brother, but I cannot go back to the palace now that I am finally free. I cannot go back there."

A shudder racks my body, and Ika wraps his arm around my shoulders, bringing me into a tight hug.

"Would you be willing to let him come here?"

"If he came alone."

"I don't think I can convince a king to go anywhere alone, but I will ensure no more than two guards, Joseph, and myself. Can you write him a letter to let him know that you are ok?" Ambrose asks.

"I'll get you something to write on, Darlin'."

"Can you read my mind now?" I ask, smiling up at Ika.

Ika chuckles, leaving the room in search of paper and a pen. I walk around to Ambrose and begin untying him from the chair.

"You seem to be processing this all relatively well, Gertrude," Ambrose states, rubbing his wrists now that they were free of their bindings.

"I think I am still in shock, and it will all hit me later," I laugh. "Honestly, I am kind of beating myself up that I didn't notice that Harrison and I were both suffering as much as the other while we lived in the same wing of the palace. I feel like a crappy sister, too focused on my own drama to look at what was going on around me."

Ika comes back with the paper, and I sit down at the table to write my letter to Harrison. Meanwhile, Ambrose and Ika have a hushed conversation, Ika giving him directions back to the palace avoiding the Silent Wood.

Once I finished writing, we readied Onyx, and, after setting and plugging his nose, Ambrose headed off with enough time to get back on the main road before nightfall. We stand on the porch, Ika pressed against my back and hugging me from behind as we watch Ambrose ride off into the forest. I stare after him long after he is no longer visible. Ika doesn't walk away, nor does he attempt to converse or move me into the house. He holds and comforts me as my mind turns today's events over and over again.

As the sun sets, I come back to the present. I turn within Ika's arms, smiling up at him. Meeting my eyes, he grins back at me.

"We're free," I whisper.

"We're free, Darlin'."

"Are you sure you want to keep me around, now that you don't have to?"

"You are my everything, Darlin'. I love you. I am not letting you go anywhere without me."

Maybe one day, I will no longer need his reassurances, but for now, it's good to be reminded I have everything I could ever want and need—my soul mate and a beautiful home to share with him forever.

Chapter Nine

HARRISON

After returning from my meeting with Charming yesterday, I locked myself in my study. The staff and court all knew not to disturb me. I have been thinking over what Charming said about Ambrose and how Kings do what *they* want. I know that doesn't always help things; my father started feuds and ongoing animosity. We were lucky it never evolved into a war. Yet, in my case, what I want is to be happy, and I think I deserve it.

I am jolted back to the present by a knock at my door. It is nine in the morning, and I don't have any meetings or obligations right now. I want to ignore them and focus on my half-formed plans, yet it is probably crucial if they are disturbing me.

"Enter," I answer in resignation.

Joseph walks in, bows, and turns to hold the door open for someone else. My breath catches in my throat as Ambrose enters the room. He is truly here in my home, in my study, looking at me. My eyes devour him, his hair is slightly longer, his body leaner, but those sky-blue eyes are the same as always. Ambrose looks as handsome as ever, dressed in a patchy brown leather riding jacket over a simple shirt and trousers. Ambrose's face has a few new smile lines around his eyes, and I feel a pang of jealousy that I wasn't the one to cause them to form. Dark circles shadow his eyes, drawing my attention to his broken nose.

Joseph stands silently, a few steps behind Ambrose, letting us take each other in, and reassuring me in Joseph's own way this is real.

"Am-Ambrose? Wh-What are you doing here?" I finally stutter out after my mind starts working again. It takes all of my self-control not to race to touch him – to confirm he is really here. I have dreamed about him showing up before, only to wake up alone with my head on my desk, my heart in my throat.

"I'm here because of your letter." He responds, unaware of my internal struggle. His voice is rich and smooth. I hadn't forgotten what his voice had sounded like over the last four years, but my memories did not do it justice. It is hard not to close my eyes and enjoy the warmth that rushes over me just from hearing his voice again.

"My letter?" He came here. He didn't write back or attend the meeting with Charming. *He came here. That's a good sign.* "Charming said that you had rushed off on another quest."

"I did."

"I-I... I don't understand."

"I received your letter... and found Gertrude."

"You what? WHAT? Where is she?"

"Not here."

My self-control is starting to wear out. My emotions are strung-out from not sleeping and the events of the last three days, and I can't understand what Ambrose is saying. Is he going to use the information of her whereabouts to manipulate me? Like Evalyn does?

"Explain," I command, needing this solved now.

"I know there is a lot to resolve between us, words unsaid, and words we regret. I need you to know, I never gave up on you, or Gertrude. I have been looking for her for the last four years." My heart starts beating faster, my mind trying to focus and understand every word. "I searched all over my kingdom and the

Jang Forest. I was beginning to give up hope of ever finding her when I received your letter yesterday morning. When I saw that you had found her with Ika and they had escaped, it was the missing piece I needed to find her. I knew Ika from when my father burned down Adaira. He was there in the aftermath of my father's destruction. I didn't know where he lived exactly, but I knew the rough whereabouts. I put that together with the knowledge of Gertrude's entrapment in the Silent Wood, and I carefully travelled through the forest, looking for any sign of his home until I found it. She gave me this letter for you."

Ambrose pulls out a letter from his jacket pocket and holds it out to me. I can see Gertrude's elegant handwriting, my eyes flicking between Ambrose and the envelope in his hands.

"Have you read it?"

"No, of course not, Baby." He replies softly.

My eyes burn with tears at the old nickname. *Kings do what they want. I just need to be brave.*

"I have missed you so much, Ro!" I exclaim, not capable of holding this in any longer, "You have no idea how sorry I am for everything that I said and did. I know there is no way for me to make it up to you, and now with you doing so much—looking for and finding Gertrude even after everything. I don't deserve you." The tears started to fall while I was talking, turning me into a sobbing mess.

Placing the letter on my desk, Ambrose walks around and pulls me into a tight hug, a hand fists my hair at the bottom of my neck and his other wraps around my waist.

"Shh, Baby. It's okay," he murmurs into my ear, placing a soft kiss on my temple. My arms hang limply at my sides, too shocked by his sudden embrace to react. Ambrose starts to pull back, but I snake my arms around him, gripping him so tightly that they ache. We embrace each other until the tears subside, his fingers run through my hair, soothing me while he breathes deeply next to my ear, allowing me to mimic his breaths and calm myself down.

I pull back from Ambrose and wipe my face, removing the last of my tears. Pulling myself together, I remember that Joseph is still in the room and saw my minor breakdown. I trust Joseph and know I don't need to worry about him gossiping about this, but I would have felt better if he hadn't witnessed it. I glance at Joseph, briefly meeting his eyes as he offers me an understanding smile.

I grimace and sit down, collecting the letter from the edge of the desk. Nodding slightly, I indicate that Ro and Joseph should sit while I unfold and begin to read Gertrude's letter.

Harrison,
There is so much going through my mind that I don't know where to start with this letter.
As I am sure Ambrose will tell you, he found me at Ika's cabin. We are putting a lot of faith in him by letting him go. I read the letter you wrote to him and genuinely believed what you said about me.
I am sorry if you feel like Ambrose betrayed your confidence in showing us the letter. We had him restrained and would not have let him go without the reassurance that we were not in danger.
Firstly, I need to reassure you if you had any doubts. It doesn't matter to me if you are gay and love Ambrose. I feel like an idiot for not being able to see it, but that goes to show how well you hid it from every-one. From your letter to Ambrose, and what little information he offered, I gather that you intended to conceal the relationship. I think the two of you make an excellent pair and are well suited to each other. I hope one day you will be as happy as I am and that you

can resolve things with Ambrose. I know that there were other factors involved in your split, but I am sorry for my inadvertent contribution to it with my disappearance. Secondly, the missing guards are in the Silent Wood. I'm sorry but we believed that you were hunting us down to either kill or return us to the prison cells, and they had us surrounded. I tricked them into following us and led them into the Silent Wood.

I understand that you want me to return to the palace, but it is not possible—not now that I am finally free of that awful place. In the throne room, when I returned, I told you that all I had ever wanted was to leave the palace and that Mother and Father never cared about or noticed me unless it was for their benefit. Well, Evalyn was worse.

When we were alone, she always treated me with disdain and disgust. Her words and actions showed me that I was beneath her notice or her care. Evalyn betrayed my confidence, manipulated me and others to benefit herself, and did anything she could to break me mentally and emotionally.

When I was younger, I was never left alone. Evalyn smothered me, trying to mould me into her perfect little puppet. After I turned sixteen, she started loosening the reins a bit, and she began to leave me alone for hours at a time. I think she believed me to be entirely under her control by then. Still, I was never allowed any friends or visitors. Evalyn conspired with Mother to manipulate me into doing what they wanted me to do and

*tricked me into believing I wanted it too. I
found it easier to be who they wanted me to
be, and I played into the character they had
created for me; it was easier to appease them
than it was to be myself.*

*I am sorry to hear that Evalyn has been
making your life hard over the last few
years. I wish I could offer you words of
advice or any weaknesses that she has that
you could use against her. I don't know what
precisely it is that Evalyn has over you, but
I suspect it has something to do with your
relationship with Ambrose. Is her power and
silence worth your unhappiness? What is her
silence doing for you? You still have her
toxic presence in your court, you are
unhappy, and you are without the person who
makes your life worth living.*

*I know we have had a lot of problems between
us in our lives, but after talking to Ambrose
and reading your letter, I think they were
mainly misunderstandings and hold no water. I
am not the person that I pretended to be in
the palace. It was a defence mechanism, and,
after reading your letter, I think that's why
you were so cruel at times, too—trying to
keep me at a distance but still wanting to
check in and care for me. I can probably
understand that better than anyone, and I am
here to talk when you are ready.*

*Ambrose begged me to come back to the palace
for you, but after reading this letter, I
hope you can understand why that isn't possible. Ambrose knows the way to the cabin; I
have told him to bring you if you choose to*

visit. I would prefer you to come alone, or with an as minimal guard as you are able.
Please come whenever you like.
Your sister,
Trudy.

I read the letter twice, as it holds so much information to process.

"Y-you told her about me? About us?" I didn't intend that to be my first question, my mouth speaking before my mind had caught up.

"I had to show her the letter. To assure her you weren't trying to trap her or throw her in a cell again." He raises his eyebrow, silently asking me about my actions, which I choose to ignore, my mind reeling.

She knows now, and she accepts me. She doesn't care. Thanks to Ambrose, we know where she is and that she is safe. He is here. He received my letter, went to find her, and then came here and held me while I cried. I couldn't take my eyes off him. My mind kept coming back to the same question. *Why?*

"Why did you do all this, Ro? Look for Gertrude for four years? Read my letter and go after her? Come here now? Why?" I can hear the desperation and pleading in my voice and want to slap myself for sounding so needy.

"There's a lot to say between us, Harry. A conversation we need to have that probably should be in private." He looks at Joseph. "No offense, but I have a feeling that you don't want to be in that conversation."

"Not particularly, no. That would be intruding." Joseph says, speaking for the first time since he entered the room. Ambrose nods solemnly and turns back to me.

"It's not what we need to discuss right now. Do you want me to take you to Gertrude? It's early enough in the day that if we leave now, we will be able to make it there by mid-afternoon."

"But—"

"But nothing. We can talk on the way or after. Gertrude is what's most important right now. I know you, and I know you will need to see her safe and to speak to her yourself before you calm down about this situation."

Thinking about her safety reminds me of what Gertrude wrote about Evalyn. Anger boils in my gut. Not only had she been making my life miserable for the last four years, but she had also been doing it to Gertrude for ten years before that? I have been thinking about how to handle Evalyn and to try to get out from under her thumb. This new information just stokes the rage growing in me. She needs to pay for the pain she has caused.

Chapter Ten

HARRISON

Conflict racks me. The desire to be close to Ambrose, with his woodsy scent and mesmerising eyes, is almost overpowering. At the same time, he is too distracting, and I need space to think. Facing Ro, I feel that little flicker of hope growing again.

"I need to be alone to think, are you able to stay?" I ask tentatively, "I want to speak with you, really, but I just need some time first, please." It's selfish of me, I know. He probably should go for his own sake. But he is a balm to the ache that has existed in my soul for the last four years, and I cannot find it in me to tell him to leave. We need to discuss where we left things, and now my only hope is to settle us back into a friendship – if nothing else. He held me as I cried and confessed that I missed him, but he never said he missed me too.

"Of course. I can wait for you in the library. It holds a lot of memories and has been a while since I have visited." He smiles his beautiful grin at me, and it heals a small part of my heart.

Remembering again that Joseph is in the room, I turn to him. His jaw is tense, like he is forcing himself to control his expression.

"Joseph, I need you to call a meeting with my advisors. Let's have it after lunch. We will meet in the usual advisors meeting chambers."

Joseph nods and bows in farewell, exiting the room and holding the door for Ambrose to follow. Ambrose hesitates, meeting my eyes again.

"I will wait however long you need me to. I am here for you; you don't have to do anything alone."

Then, he too left the room.

There's a silence so loud I could hear my ears ringing. I stand staring after him, trying to control my breathing and think about anything other than Ambrose being in the palace. *Concentrate, goddamn it!* My breath quickens, speeding up until I am struggling to breathe properly. I feel like the walls are caving in on me. So much has happened within the course of a few days it is overwhelming me, and I notice the signs of a panic attack. I had only ever had one before, after the fiasco with Ambrose when Gertrude went missing. *Space!* I need space and fresh air to think and calm down! The second the thought forms, I am tearing out of my study and rushing out into the gardens.

Walking with no real direction in the gardens, I wander up and down paths while taking deep breaths and trying to sort my mind out. As my legs began to tire, I sit down on the bench at the lake. It's funny how walking without direction has led me here. An hour passed with me trying – and failing – to process everything. What would Ro think about how long I was taking?

"No! Focus Harrison! You just started to calm down. Don't think about him yet. Get everything else sorted out first," I chastise myself aloud, needing to hear the words to redirect my thoughts.

Gertrude. We know where she is, so why am I still here? Why aren't I going to her now? Oh, right. Evalyn. She, along with our mother, had made Gertrude's life here so miserable that she didn't even want to come home.

Dealing with Evalyn is my priority before I can even think about going to Gertrude or resolving things with Ambrose.

Resolve things with Ambrose? One mention of him and our situation becomes my focus again, derailing my progress.

Does his return mean that he is not totally disgusted with me? Do I still have a chance to be with him? Charming's words from Adaira flash through my mind.

"You are a king, Harrison! Last time I checked, they do whatever they wanted and fucked off anyone who disagreed with them. Take that leaf out of our fathers' book if nothing else, do what you want, do what will make you happy. Everyone else can either fall in line or leave."

I never liked the idea of having my self-worth depend on other people's remarks, yet I allowed it to happen, absorbing the flippant words as they distorted my self-image. Charming's words had burrowed down into my soul.

I am gay, and I am okay with it. I never fought it, or tried to change myself, so why can't I tell everyone else? I don't need to be singing it from the rooftops, but I can show myself that I am proud of who I am. Warmth fills me as I realise I actually am happy with who I am and that I deserve happiness.

As king, as well as when I was crown prince, I've always put my duty first. I had to put the interests of Daes first, and my happiness last. I have let people like Evalyn and my father manipulate the way I viewed myself. I am ashamed to have let them sway me. I had fallen into a depression that stemmed from my view of myself.

It doesn't vanish the moment I accept myself, but with ongoing work, I *will* beat it.

Now, I need to pull myself together and show Ambrose that he is worth everything to me. He is worth my crown, my kingdom, everything. He is more important to me than anything else. With that startling insight, I jump to my feet and make my way back to the palace. I need him to know now, this second. I had already wasted four years of our lives over trivial drama, and even longer pretending he wasn't my world.

Standing in the library doorway, I see him sitting in a small reading nook amongst the fiction novels. I wait a moment to admire him from the doorway. Still, in the same clothes as earlier, he looks tired and weary. No matter how relaxed he looks, he would always be deadly after all his training. It's hard to surprise him, which makes me even more interested in how he broke his nose. His black hair is pointing at all angles as if he had been pulling on it in distress. He sits with his ass slid to the edge of the seat, his feet propped on the table, a book held in his lap. He manages to look both at home and out of place, and I have to suppress a laugh.

A memory of our teenage years in the library resurfaces. Ambrose had been sitting in the same spot and position that he is in now. We had been hosting his family for an overnight stay, and Ambrose and I had snuck out for a late-night meeting in the library. I had arrived to find him bunkered down and reading a book. Deciding to play on the memory, I walk towards him and repeat the same words to him I had said so long ago.

"I would wager that you have a nice bookworm," I say in a low murmur. My voice has gotten deeper since we were teenagers.

Ambrose's eyes heat as they meet mine, two large pools of desire drowning me in their depths.

"Come over here, Baby, and I'll show you just how *nice* it is."

Baby. A simple four-letter word that has me melting, every single time.

"Here goes nothing," I mutter to myself, sitting opposite him.

Chapter Eleven

AMBROSE

Harry shocked me reciting that old line; I had forgotten about it. I have been in the library waiting for him for about two hours now, and it felt like I had been sitting on nails. But his acknowledgement of our time spent here relaxes me, the tension in my shoulders ebbing away.

Harry sits down opposite me, exhaustion radiating off of him.

"How are you?" I ask tentatively. "You have had to deal with a lot over the last few days. How are you handling it?"

"Not well, honestly." He laughs self-deprecatingly. "I have made some bad decisions based on what others wanted, and it is all catching up with me. I have allowed my mind, opinions, and actions to be manipulated and distorted by others. I am not proud of who I became. I have been rude and cruel, acting before thinking." He sighs and sinks back into his seat. "My citizens say I am mad, and I finally proved them right. Gertrude finally came home after four years, Ro. Four fucking years, and I threw her into a cell! I am ashamed of myself. For that, for not trusting you, for not believing you, for not allowing myself to be happy and to do what is best for me." He breaks off, looking away from me.

Bridging the distance between us, I step over the small table, scoop Harry up, and sit down, cradling him in my lap.

"I know, Baby, I know. We can fix it; it will be okay." I whisper into his ear while stroking his hair, soothing him as much as myself. I had dared to hope I would hold him again. After four years apart, I would take any touch I could get.

"I'm sorry, Ambrose." His voice is raspy from and muffled by my chest as he hides his face. "Crying on you in my study, and now this…"

"There's nothing to be ashamed of, Baby. Sometimes we all need to cry—it's okay. I am glad I was there to hold you and help you through it, and to hold you now."

Harry tilts his head back to look at me. "After all that I have done and failed to do, how are you still here waiting for me?"

"I love you, Harrison."

"You still love me?" He asks, shock lacing his voice.

"I have been in love with you for most of my life, Baby. I have never been able to picture my life without you in it. The last four years have killed me—all I wanted to do was reach out and talk to you, to try and fix everything. I knew I had to find Gertrude first, though. After everything that my family did, I had to fix what I could before returning to you." I feel tears sting the back of my eyelids. Harry sits there, staring at me, a mixture of awe and surprise on his face.

"I don't understand… How do you not hate or despise me? After everything, I said to you in the gardens, in the maze, after turning you down *twice*. Why would you need to fix things? I was the one in the wrong. I am the one who screwed everything up."

"I could never hate you," I say. "I have not been with anyone else in the last four years, even with everything that happened between us."

"Well, I haven't either, but that doesn't mean—"

There was no point in this debate. I cut Harrison off—sliding my hand up, I cup the back of his neck and, pulling his face to mine, I smash our lips together. It is the first time our lips touched in four years. Harrison's mouth is still, but his fingers curl in my shirt. My mouth moulds to his, kissing his mouth thoroughly, then I kiss his upper and lower lips in turn. I am about to pull back when Harry finally comes to life in my arms.

Pouncing forward, his hands cup my jaw, fingers scratching against the stubble there, and he kisses me back. Pressing me back into the chair, Harry lavishes my mouth in hot, messy kisses. Pushing his tongue into my mouth, deepening our kiss, he moans as he squirms in my lap. My hands drop to his waist, assisting him as he twists to straddle me. Flashes of heat flutter through me as his hard cock brushes against mine.

"Wait, Baby, wait for a second," I panted, gripping his hips tighter to halt his movements.

Harry's face crumples, looking to the side, he leans back.

"I'm sorry. Let me up," Harry says, sadly.

"That's not what I meant," I say, but I do drop my hands from his hips—giving him the freedom to move if he chooses too.

"Then what?" his head whips back around to look at me. He doesn't get off.

"You heard me; I told you I love you."

"I love you too, but I also am awaiting an explanation." Harry replies sassily.

I press a soft kiss on the corner of his mouth.

"For a few reasons. I feel like I'm taking advantage of you while you're looking for some comfort. The last conversation we had about 'us' ended with you saying that you would always love me but couldn't be with me."

Is it weak of me to need his reassurance that this is more than a lapse in judgement? Probably. Do I need to hear him admit it anyway? Unfortunately, yes, yes, I do.

"Ro!" he exclaims, cupping my cheek, "You are my everything. I have missed you so terribly. I have replayed that day over and over in my head a thousand times, trying to figure out how I could fix everything between us."

Those words are a balm to my broken heart, piecing me back together and settling the insecurities I had harboured since that damn party all those years ago.

"So, that's settled—can we continue now?" Harry shifts in my lap, bumping our noses together.

"Well, there's multiple reasons." I rest my hands on his hips, counting on my fingers against his side. "We are in the library in the middle of the day where anyone could walk in and see us. You also told Joseph to organise a meeting of your advisors, which I am assuming is soon. And we have more to talk about."

"I suppose you are right. Why do you have to be so reasonable?" He grumbles.

"Sometimes, I ask myself the same thing," I mutter as he moves in my lap again, causing our now semi-hard cocks to press together. Instinctively, my hips thrust up into him while my hands pull him down to grind into me. I moan at the amazing feeling of his dick against mine.

Voice husky, Harry leans forward and presses his kiss-swollen lips to my ear, his tongue darting out to flick my lobe, "We need to stop, remember?"

"Ugh," I whimper. "You should probably get off my lap for that to be successful." Reluctantly, I let go, and he stands and sits in my vacated chair. "So, what are you going to talk to your advisors about?"

Harrison deeply inhales as if gathering courage. Meeting my eyes, he exhales, "I am going to tell them that I am gay."

"What?" I manage to choke out.

"I am going to come out as gay to the court, the kingdom."

"You are?"

"Ambrose, I need you to know I am not coming out because of you or because of us."

I feel like he punched me in the gut. I can't help but feel like he's about to say he doesn't want me—I know he just said the opposite, but being here with him is so fresh, so new. It's easier to believe it's about to vanish than that he's really here.

"What does that mean?" I snap, and I instantly regret it. "I just—" I say, trying again. "What are you saying?"

"All I'm saying is—" There's a crack in his voice. "I want there to be no guilt or pressure on you to do the same. I don't presume to know what you think now—after all this time things could have changed for you. I am coming out because I have been miserable, not only for the last four years without you, but I have hidden who I am from practically everyone my entire life." His voice steadies, determination flowing out of him, "I want to be me, and I want to be happy." He takes my hand. "You knew the version of myself that was best for me all those years ago—a man who is open and unafraid. I'm finally trying to be that man."

"What are you saying, Harry? That I can go back to being your little secret if I want to?" I sneer.

"I never saw you that way," he replies apologetically. "You are everything to me, Ro. I am saying that I am yours in any capacity. If you want to be friends or if you want to be secret lovers while you marry a woman or if you want to be out with me. It is your choice. I want you to make it without any pressure, to have all the information before you made your decision."

"You are an idiot, you know?"

"I know, I allowed my family and Evalyn to manipulate me—"

"That's not why you are an idiot, Harry."

"Then—"

"You are an idiot, my beautiful Harry, for thinking that I wouldn't want to be open with you." Standing, I step over the table, grabbing his hands and pulling him up to stand with me, "I want to be there for you, with you. You are mine, Harry. You have always been mine; I won't let you go again."

Cupping his face, I pull his mouth to mine, no longer caring that we are out in the open for anyone to see. He is my Baby, my love, and he is finally giving us the chance to claim each other.

Chapter Twelve

HARRISON

We kiss for what feels like hours until we are breathless and aching for more. If I had the time, I would drag Ambrose to my chambers now and give us both what we are desperate to have. Unfortunately, I have a meeting and responsibilities to complete first. I reluctantly pull back from Ro's embrace.

"Is that a yes then? Are you okay with me coming out? Can you give us a second chance?" I sound needy and desperate, but hell if I'm not. Ro is the one person I have always been able to be completely myself with, no pretences or expectations. I have no desire to hide who I am from him.

"You are my heart. Of course, I will support you." He runs the tip of his nose down the bridge of mine, leaning in for more kisses.

"Wait, Ro," I chuckle, "I need to go to my meeting."

"Did you want me to join you?" He asks huskily.

"Although it would be great to have you there for moral support, I feel like if you were there, I would be too distracted."

"After?"

"After."

We share one last lingering kiss, and I leave him to go to my meeting.

* * *

I enter my advisors meeting chambers to see everyone gathered and waiting for me. By the time I arrived, I look presentable and washed the tears and kisses from my face.

In attendance are Evalyn, Joseph, Count Drew, Sir Sil, Sir Duncan, Lord Jay, and Fredrick. They were my father's advisors that I had inherited along with the throne. They stand and bow as I enter the room and walk to my chair. It isn't as elegant as my throne, but it is far more comfortable and seats me at the head of our meeting table.

"Thank you all for meeting me today at such short notice," I begin. The advisors live in the court apartments and are at my beck and call for meetings such as this. "Now, we have a few things to discuss today."

"Is everything ok, Your Majesty? Have there been new developments with King Charming?" Evalyn asks.

"Yes, Evalyn. Not only has new information come to light, but our circumstances and stance have altered."

All eyes fixed upon me, everyone being smart enough to hold their tongues, waiting for me to continue. It is so quiet I can hear them shifting in their seats.

"Firstly," I begin, my deep voice echoing around the stone room, "Princess Gertrude was located, she is safe, unharmed and was not taken by King Charming."

"Are you sure?" Sir Sil asks brazenly.

"Quite sure. I have seen the Princess but have not spoken with her at length yet. I have spoken to King Charming—"

"YOU WHAT?" Evalyn's screeches cut me off. "Why would you speak with him without consulting anyone? He could be tricking you."

"Shut your mouth, Evalyn. I am the King; you DO NOT speak over me." I command.

Her lips twist in displeasure, and I can feel her discontent building—time to get this over with before she can throw it out there.

"Secondly, there is more information that you need to know, and I believe, will receive better coming directly from me. I am gay. I have no intention of taking a Queen. I have hidden this from the Kingdom for too long, and I am now informing you all."

I look into the faces of each person present. Drew, Sil, Duncan, Jay, and Fredrick look surprised, and thankfully not disapprovingly. Joseph looks relieved.

Evalyn looks murderous.

Chapter Thirteen

AMBROSE

I watch Harry leave the library and wait a few minutes. Then I follow him. Harry is already seated in the room with his advisors when I arrive to find an open door as if knowing I would linger outside to listen. I take up a position next to the door, leaning against the cobblestone wall, listening to their conversation.

"Most of you don't look displeased, so I think some of you may not object to this." Harry addresses the group, "I do not believe that me being out will need to change anything for Daes. I am the same man that I have always been. Only now I intend to be true to who I am. If any of you have a problem with it, you can leave this court."

I tense. I need to let Harry fight his own battles, but I want to run in and defend him.

Everyone maintains their silence.

"You can speak now," Harrison prompts.

"I have no problem with it, Your Majesty," Joseph offers.

"Thank you, Joseph. If anyone does have a problem, you need to speak up now. I will be issuing a statement tomorrow to the kingdom. All the citizens will be made aware of the situation."

My pride for him blossoms in my chest. This man, this

wonderful, magnificent man, he is mine, and I cannot wait to claim him in front of the world.

"Right then," Harry continues. There must have been non-verbal agreements that I couldn't see from my position. "Lastly, I am dismissing Evalyn from her position within my court."

"WHAT?" Evalyn exclaims.

I plant my feet, forcing myself to stay still and not rush into the room.

"You heard me, Evalyn. Joseph will escort you from the palace. You can return to the life you had before you joined us."

"I have been here for fifteen years! I do not deserve to be thrown out like trash! I have given everything to you and your family."

"You have been cruel, vicious, and vindictive. You abused Princess Gertrude for eight years."

"I never! Did she tell you that? That ungrateful cow! You all know how selfish that girl was! She has been gone for four years, and now you are going to throw me out on her say so?"

"This is how you speak to your king? Of your princess? A girl that you helped raise and care for, for eleven years?"

"What did she tell you?" Evalyn asks, ignoring his questions.

"You are not privy to that information. What I am saying is, you need to gather your things and leave. I will allow you the time to stay the night and get your affairs in order. A guard will watch you for the remainder of your time here."

"This is ridiculous! Your Mother and Father would be disgusted by your behaviour. What am I to do?"

"Be honest for once in your life, Evalyn. The real reason you are upset is that I have taken away the power you held over me for the last four years, the only reason that you are still here. You found out I was gay and used that to manipulate me. Now the world will know, and you won't be able to sway me any longer. That is why you are angry."

"You are a disgusting man; how can you disrespect your

father and your ancestors with your sick and twisted ways. You are foul, perverted—"

"ENOUGH!" Harry bellows. "I will no longer permit you to speak to me in such manner. I have already dismissed you. Leave the room now before I have Joseph escort you out."

"How can you all be supportive of this?" Evalyn continues. "This pansy cannot lead this kingdom in the right direction. I will not leave; you cannot make me. This palace is MY home! After everything I have done to get here, I will not just give it up. I endured sleeping with your father to gain a position in his court, and what did I get? Looking after that filthy sister of yours. I bow and scrape and finally rangled a better position, and now you think you can take it away from me?"

A loud scuffle sounds as a chair is pushed back and tips onto the floor. No longer content to stand guard in the hall, I rush into the room to see Evalyn running to Harry. Joseph pushes off from his position against the wall and reaches out to Evalyn.

I watch in slow motion as she pulls a dagger from the bodice of her dress—fear courses through me. *I am not going to reach him in time.* I should have been next to him for the meeting, and then I could be there and do something. Evalyn raises her dagger as she approaches—Harry sits frozen in his chair. Her violent reaction completely surprised him.

One second, Evalyn is standing over Harry, dagger poised to slice his neck; the next, Joseph is behind her, the blade of his sword protruding from her chest. One moment she was about to take my world away from me; the next, her blood had splattered the table and Harry, her lifeless body dropping to the ground.

With eyes only for Harry, I rush to his side, yanking him out of his chair and wrapping my arms around him, pressing his body against mine.

"Oh my God, Baby. That was too close. Are you okay?" I murmur into his ear, rubbing my hands up and down his back. I am not sure if I am trying to soothe him or myself.

"I'm ok, Ro. She didn't even touch me—"

"She almost did! I almost lost you—after finally getting you back, she almost took you from me, again!" I am on the verge of tears just at the thought of losing him, "I cannot live without you, Baby, don't make me do it again, please." I am apparently not too proud to beg.

"I am never letting you go again," Harry assured me, tilting his head to press a kiss to my lips. It was chaste and not enough to satisfy the hunger within me. I followed his mouth as he pulled away, needing more. More kisses, more touches, just more of Harrison. My Harrison.

"Uh, Ro," Harry whispers, pressing his hand against my mouth, gently pushing away my advance, "We aren't alone."

"Fuck." I whisper, realising I had just put on quite a show.

Harry chuckles. Caught up in the moment, we had both forgotten we were in a room filled with members of his court.

"Precisely," he whispers.

Reluctantly, I release him from my embrace, and we turn to face his advisors. We are met with smiles and knowing glances. I take a deep breath and feel the lingering tension leave Harry's body.

Harry addresses the room. "Well, everyone, as I am sure you all know, this is Prince Ambrose. I am hoping that you will all be seeing a lot of him in the future." Laughter erupts through the room, calming us both.

"Why didn't I do this sooner?" he murmurs to me. "I feel so free now."

Chapter Fourteen

HARRISON

The meeting ended as my advisors left congratulating and accepting me, accepting us. I hadn't known what I was walking into, but I honestly didn't expect that to happen.

I had seen death before, witnessing Mother and Father dying, but watching Evalyn get killed was a new experience for me. I had never seen such a violent act. Not that I blamed Joseph for killing her; he was doing his duty to protect me, as King and as a friend.

The guards quietly removed Evalyn's body. I would need to contact any family Evalyn had and advise them of her treason and consequential death. After I finish that duty, and as soon as I can get away, I will have Ro take me to Gertrude. Even with everything that has passed between us, I need to see her, to settle our differences in person, and to put the past behind us.

"Well, King Harrison," Ro's husky, sultry voice draws me to him. We are the only ones still in the meeting room. "Now that business is handled, what would you like to do?"

Bliss momentarily overwhelms me. We finally have the chance to do anything we want.

"How about a tour of the palace?"

Ambrose's bright smile fades into faint disappointment.

"I have already seen the palace several times, Harry, why do I need a tour?"

"I think there are a few things you haven't seen before that you're going to start seeing a lot more of." I grin ferally, trying to give him a hint.

"I had other things in mind, but I suppose we can get to that later. Lead on, Harry. I'm assuming you're the tour guide?" His smile returns, and we leave the room, walking side by side, hand in hand, down the hallways of my home.

"I am afraid you are stuck with me."

I lead Ro towards the King's Quarters, a wing of the palace I had renovated after my father's death, turning it into space for me rather than a source of sad memories. We walk in silence, just enjoying the feeling of being together. When we approach the large oak doors that separate the rest of the palace from my rooms, I pull gently on Ro's arm to halt him.

"Do you know where we are?" I ask in a whisper, and the air feels rigid with the sexual tension growing between us.

"In front of two large doors?" he answers sarcastically.

I chuckle. "Why don't you open the doors then and see where we are for yourself?" I release his hand.

I notice that guards had followed us from the meeting room, but they fanned out, leaving us relatively alone. When I had redesigned this part of the palace, I cut off any external entrance points. At the time, we were afraid of any retaliation from King Kryler and Prince Charming and did not want to allow for any possible risks. That being the case, it also ensured that I did not need to have guards enter my quarters. The only people allowed inside were Joseph and a handful of maids that had been cleared and monitored.

Ambrose opens the doors tentatively and walks into the room. I follow one step behind him, studying his profile as he takes in the space around us, and allowing the doors to close behind us—leaving us completely alone. The doors open into a long hallway, with the rooms breaking off like tree branches. We pass the entertainment room which holds a large bookcase and desk in the corner, a billiard table, and a small collection of musical instruments.

"More books? Why do you need these along with the library?"

"These are my favourites; I like to have them on hand for light reading and distraction."

"Is this what you wanted to show me then? A private collection of books?" he asks, a little confused.

"No," I chuckle. "Our tour's not done yet."

We leave the entertainment room and continue down the hallway. At the end of the hall, there's nowhere to go except into a closed door. His hand stretches for the handle, twisting and slowly opening it into my bedroom.

Whenever we visited each other, we always stayed in a guest room. We never even entered each other's bedrooms.

To have him here now, I feel peace settle over me. This moment is how it should be. Nothing that feels this perfect, pure, and wonderful could ever be wrong.

I watch Ro's eyes grow big with realisation, quickly studying the space. He turns to me, and I run my eyes over his body, my gaze zeroing in on the desire in his eyes.

"Your room?" Ro asks, his voice husky with desire, "You wanted to show me your room?"

"Yes," I confirm.

"You said this is a tour for me to get familiar with rooms that I will use a lot in the future."

"I did."

"Does that mean..." He froze.

"Ambrose, I have loved you for as long as I have known you. Over the last ten years, we have stolen kisses, blow jobs, and private moments where time has allowed. I once told you that I would not let you take me until we could be somewhere we didn't have to worry about noise," I begin undoing the buttons on my shirt, removing it to bare my torso to him, "about who else could be walking around the garden beds, or who could catch us." My eyes focus on his face as I begin stepping out of my shoes. He audibly gulps, frozen from watching me slowly remove my clothing.

Standing with only trousers on, I stalk to him and cup his jaw in my hand, tilting his head down to mine.

"I want more, Ro. I want everything with you. Actually, I'm pretty sure I need it. I have longed for you for so long, I know I won't be able to continue if I don't feel you in me."

Unable to hold back any longer, my lips crash into his. Heated and feverish kisses consume me as Ro's hands run up my bare back. All of the times we have been intimate, we had to rush, remain partially clothed out of fear, and filled with teenage hormones.

Now we had all the time in the world and the chance to remove clothes, to see each other.

Ro's kisses move down my throat, licking my skin. His nose tickles my neck, inhaling my scent.

"You have too many clothes on." I breathe out harshly, lifting my hands to his shirt. I claw at the buttons, tearing them open and yanking his shirt from his shoulders. It pools around his elbows, forcing him to release me to allow his shirt to fall to the floor. His lips come back to mine, tongue snaking in, hypnotising me. My hands lift to his chest, playing softly in the hair there. My fingers trail lightly over his nipples and send a shiver down his spine.

Ro moves to my ear, sucking the lobe into his mouth, drawing a loud moan from me.

"Take off my pants, Harry," he mutters.

Hastily, I drop my hands to his trousers and undo them. I fall to my knees reverently in front of him, helping him step out of his shoes and his pants, leaving him in his underwear.

When I looked up at him, I see the hunger in his eyes. I am sure I have never seen anything more erotic.

"Take them off," he orders me. I obey, hooking my thumbs

into the waistband and dragging them down past his hips. His hard cock was caught in his underpants momentarily before flicking up and slapping against his lower stomach. I stare unabashedly at his cock, mesmerized by his long, hard length.

Torn between taking him into my mouth and taking my clothes off, I struggle to do both. Licking the head, I undo my pants and push them and my underpants down my thighs, allowing my aching cock to hang free.

"Mm, Baby. I have missed having your mouth on me." Ro says as I suck his cock into my mouth. Letting it pop out, I look back up at him.

"I've missed your cock in my mouth," I say, licking up his shaft and placing it back into my hot, wet mouth. Small grunts and groans escape his mouth, jolting straight through me to my cock. Nothing has ever turned me on more than bringing Ro pleasure.

Suddenly, Ro reaches down and pulls me up to stand next to him. "If you keep doing that, I am not going to last very long." He mutters between sloppy kisses.

"Do you need to?"

"I would like to get the chance to love you before I cum."

"Do you remember when we were teenagers? We had done a fair amount of planning our sex life together."

Impossibly his gaze heats more, "I remember, Baby. Did you want me to do what we talked about?" Speechless, I nod my agreement. Taking my hand, Ro leads me over to the bed and has me kneel in the middle of the bed, facing away from him. He kneels behind me and pushes on my back until I am on my hands and knees, ass in the air, an offer to him.

With a hand on each cheek, I can feel his hot breath on my lower back as he drops a kiss at the top of my ass. He places soft, lingering kisses on each cheek before dropping to lick my entrance. The heat of his mouth is quickly replaced by the scorching feel of his tongue, darting out to circle my tight hole.

Whimpering shamelessly, I wriggle, needing slightly more from him and arching into his rough hands.

He grips me tighter, halting my squirming as he spits onto me, moving one of his hands to massage it into my hole.

His head drops to suck one of my balls into his mouth while his finger pushes into me.

"Ah!" I exclaim in surprise. Slowly and carefully, he moves his finger within me, withdrawing until just the tip of his finger remains then plunging back into my depths. Ro pulls his head back to watch his finger fucking my ass and spits on my hole again, lubricating and stretching my entrance. Inserting another finger, he twists his body, laying on the bed with his head between my legs, allowing him to take my cock into his mouth.

Unintelligible noises escape my mouth—I am unable to hold them in with the amount of pleasure coursing through my body. My cock slides in and out of Ro's mouth, his tongue is licking from the base to the head, groaning at the taste of my pre-cum. Vibrations course through me—I can feel my cock harden in his mouth. Having my cock deep in his mouth while his fingers are in me is fantastic—the only thing better would be having his cock in me. I know that is coming next—Ambrose's mouth and hands on me, mixed with anticipation, builds the orgasm within me. His finger presses against my prostate, and I explode.

Chapter Fifteen

AMBROSE

I capture all of his cum, holding it in my mouth, disregarding the pain from breathing through my nose, stroking until I gather every last drop. I forgot how he tasted, and having him in my mouth again now is a heady experience. I want nothing more than to swallow his load, to savour every drop, but I have plans for this. We planned this out when Harry had turned eighteen, hoping that we would be able to act it out one day. I am glad we now have the chance.

Managing to keep most of his cum in my mouth, I slide his now softening cock from my mouth and ease out from underneath Harry. Manoeuvring without withdrawing my fingers from his ass, I position myself on my knees behind him on the bed again.

Harry looks over his shoulder, and our eyes meet before dropping to where my fingers still move slowly within him. I feel his watchful gaze as I purse my lips, allowing his cum to drip down to the top of his crack, trickling down to his hole, meeting my hand.

I keep moving my fingers, adding a third as he loosens more, accepting me into his body. I twist my hand, entering his hole from a different angle and pressing on his prostate again. Harry has good stamina, and with a little more encouragement, he will be hard for me again. I spit the remaining cum into my left hand, lowering it down to my cock, slicking it up.

"Your cum on my cock feels amazing, Baby." I groan, meeting his eyes over his shoulder again, the heat and love I can see in them almost knocks me over.

"Do it, Ro. Please don't make me beg. I need you in me."

Those words reverberate through me, my need for him meeting his.

Withdrawing my hand, I line myself up, and we both moan as I rub my head against his entrance.

"I wish I could draw this out, bring you to the edge again and again. Not letting you cum, making you lose control, and beg me." I say, pressing into him, watching his ass stretch over my cock. "That will have to wait for next time. I need to be in your ass."

Moans and grunts escape us as I slowly ease myself within him, not stopping until there is no space between us.

"That's all of me, Baby—you have all of me in this tight, delicious ass of yours." I slap his ass cheek, causing him to flinch slightly and tense around my cock.

"Ohh, Ro!" Harry moans, and I start to move my cock inside him. Alternating between hard, deep thrusts and soft, shallow teasing.

Suddenly, I pull out, causing Harry to yelp softly in displeasure.

"Where are you going?" he asks, turning to look at me.

"I want to watch your face when I make love to you, Baby. Do you want to lay on your back or ride me?"

"Ride you, please, can I ride you?" he begs.

I chuckle, "You don't have to ask me twice."

He shifts around on the bed, allowing me to lay down in the middle and giving him space to straddle my lap. My hands instantly seek out his hips, using my hold to grind his body against my throbbing erection.

"Oh, yes, Baby. You feel so good."

Using my stomach as a hand hold, Harry lifts himself enough so my cock can slide back into him, and we moan in unison.

Leaning down, he presses his lips to mine, angling his body so I can thrust up into him as we kiss. Our tongues rub against each other, twisting and tangling. My hands grip his hips, slamming his body down onto my cock. I break the kiss, and Harry moves his mouth down to nip at my neck.

"I don't think I am going to last much longer, Baby." I pant both from exertion and being on the edge of exploding in him.

"Cum in this ass, Ambrose." He purrs against my neck. "Mark me. Make me yours in every way."

His words undo something in me, unleashing a man I had forgotten existed. I roll us over—somehow managing it without slipping out of him—and hover above him.

"You have always been mine, Harrison Daes. You will always be mine," I declare, thrusting into him. I wrap my hand around his pulsating cock, feeling he is close too. I jerk him fast, keeping my grip tight, rubbing the head of his cock with the pad of my thumb before sliding down again. Simultaneously filling him and jerking him sets us both off, and we cum in unison. My cum fills his depths while his splatters on both of us.

Trying to be gentle, I pull out of his ass and flop onto the bed next to him, exhausted. Harry rolls into my side and snuggles his way under my arm, leaning his head against my shoulder.

"Worth the wait," he murmurs, closing his eyes on the verge of sleep.

"Baby," I chuckle, "We need to clean up."

"In a minute."

* * *

*I*t was not a minute. It was a few hours. We had both fallen asleep and awoken to Joseph knocking on the door, alerting us that dinner would be ready in fifteen minutes.

Harry is the king, so of course, they would hold dinner for him, but we both knew we needed refuelling after our crazy afternoon and missing lunch.

We quickly cleaned up before heading down to the dining room. We enter the dining room to find a very intimate and romantic place setting. The usual eight-seater round table was replaced with a smaller table, large enough for only two people. There was a deep red tablecloth covering the table, matching napkins, and a vase of red and white roses—the room is lit only with the candles on the table's candelabra and the fireplace.

I turn to Harrison. "Did you plan all this?" I ask in astonishment.

"As much as I wish I could take credit for this romantic gesture, I cannot. I didn't do this."

The footman enters and encourages us both to sit down, pouring us glasses of red wine. Then he leaves us alone in the room.

"To our future," I raise my glass. We toast, our glasses clinking together, and we drink.

A radiant smile spreads across Harry's lips. I am torn between wanting to see his smile and kissing those still swollen lips. But his smile quickly falls and is replaced with a look of torment.

"I need to see Gertrude, Ambrose."

"I know, we will speak with Joseph after dinner and organise for you to travel as soon as possible."

Our conversation is interrupted by the footman returning to serve us a delicious meal: Baked potatoes and vegetables with roast beef. After serving, he leaves us alone again.

"I think this might be your staff's way of accepting this," I say, indicating the two of us.

"Our staff." Harrison corrects me.

"Our staff?"

"As I said earlier, I hope you will be here a lot in the future. We have missed time to make up for, and I would like for you to move in here as soon as you are willing." He says it hesitantly, all traces of the kingly bravado gone. It is just my Harry, full of nerves asking me to live with him.

"Immediately then." I grin.

Relief eases his features. We fall into an easy conversation for the remainder of the meal, discussing what we have been doing for the last four years.

I had hoped, but I never truly believed we would ever be here.

"Not too far now, only another hundred meters or so," Ambrose says, turning to me from his seat atop Onyx.

We are in the Jang Forest, almost at Ika's cabin. It was an easy decision, coming to see Gertrude, and we began planning after dinner last night. Following dinner, we spoke with Joseph, asking him to arrange today's travelling party. Along with myself and Ambrose, Joseph, and two other guards accompanied us. I have been racked with nervous anticipation all morning.

Well, almost all morning. Nothing, absolutely nothing, can compare to the feeling of sleeping cuddled up with Ambrose, wrapped around each other all night, and then waking in his arms. Looking at him now, I can feel those emotions stirring within me again. I am the luckiest man in the world, having this man's love and heart.

After four years apart, another person may have been more demanding, needing more things from me, whether that be time or commitments. Not my Ambrose, he was quick to help me get to Gertrude and made no complaints about leaving our warm bed. He knew me, and it feels good knowing he has forgiven me for the mistakes that I have made. We have both grown, changed, and evolved. There is nothing in this world that I cannot do with him at my side, and I will do everything in my power to keep him by my side for the rest of our lives.

I had planned to address the kingdom and contact Evalyn's family today. However, Sir Duncan stepped in and told me he would take care of the address while I went to visit Gertrude.

Our journey through the Jang Forest was quick and relatively easy, with Ambrose's experience there combined with the information Ika imparted. We were able to skirt the Silent Wood and are now almost upon Ika's clearing. I have several things I want to say to Gertrude, and I spent the journey here running statements and sentences through my mind.

Ambrose reaches out and grabs my hand, "It will be ok, Harry. I will be here for you if you need me."

I squeeze his hand, comforted by his touch, and urge my horse forward. Breaking through the edge of the trees, we enter a large rectangular clearing. Spring is starting to turn the dead grass green, and budding flowers shoot from the ground. There are two buildings at the opposite end of the clearing, and Ambrose leads us towards the cabin. I hesitate a moment before dismounting, taking the time to fix my hair and straighten my clothes before walking around my horse to the cabin steps. Joseph follows behind us, leaving the other two guards to stay with the horses.

As my foot lands on the bottom step, the cabin door swings open. Ika stands stiffly in the middle of the doorway, and Gertrude peeks out from his side.

"Gertrude," I sigh, full of relief, remorse, and something else I cannot quite name. Gertrude steps out from behind Ika. His arm wraps around her waist, and he anchors her to his side.

"Hello, Harrison, Ambrose." She nods at each of us.

"I don't know if you remember me, Miss," Joseph starts.

"Yes, I do, Joseph." Gertrude says with a small smile, cutting off the rest of Joseph's statement, "I know you need to inspect the cabin before you allow the King inside. We will stay out here with these guards." She is clear and direct, not unlike how she was before she went missing... was stuck in the Silent Wood—and yet, she is no longer distant. Her face and voice are full of emotion, showcasing how much this experience has changed her. "I am the daughter of a King, you know; I do remember how these things work. Like it happened, oh, I don't know," she smirks up at Ika, and I see pure joy radiating off him as he looks down at her, "last week."

Joseph laughs softly and shows himself into the house, taking his time to check everything and deem it safe from risks. I struggle to find my voice; Ambrose clasps my hand in his and pulls me up the stairs. I realise then that I haven't moved since the door was opened.

"Thank you for allowing us to return, Gertrude," Ambrose says, finding the words when I have none.

"Please, call me Trudy. I prefer it to Gertrude." She scrunches up her face, reminding me of when we were children, and she was more carefree.

"You are really here," I utter, voice strained.

"Yes, Harrison, I am here."

"I half expected you would run and hide once you knew I would come."

Trudy laughs, "I may have once upon a time, but this is my home now, Harrison. Not even you would be capable of driving me out of it."

Joseph returns at that moment, giving me the approval to enter the cabin.

"Would you like some tea?" Ika asks.

"Uh, yes, please." I didn't take him to be the type to cook or wait on others. In a daze, I follow Ambrose and the others into the cabin. Hardly glancing around the space, I sit across from Trudy at the dining table.

There is something unusual about this whole encounter, and I cannot put my finger on it. We wait in silence as Ika makes tea, then joins us at the table. Trudy and I stare at one another, studying each other's faces.

You can do what you want, you only need to be brave.

Brave. I think to myself.

"Did you mean what you said, in your letter Trudy?" I ask.

She lets out a breath that she had been holding, "Yes, Harrison. Every word." A tear suddenly falls from the corner of her eye, and she rushes to wipe it away. I saw it, though. In an instant, I am out of my chair and rounding the table. Ika tenses as I pull Trudy from her chair, and before he has the chance to say anything, I have Trudy wrapped in my arms, hugging my sister for the first time since we were children. A sob racks through me, and I feel her shake with her own tears.

"I am sorry, Trudy. I am so sorry for everything I did."

"I understand, Harrison. We were both products of our upbringing. We didn't have control over what we were like."

"I still shouldn't have locked you up. I should have welcomed you with open arms and rejoiced that you were home."

"It's not my home, Harrison. I cannot live there anymore, not now that I finally got out of that hellish place," she says.

"She's gone, Trudy."

"She... who... what...?" She stammers, confusion twisting her features as she pulls back from my embrace to look up at me.

"Evalyn, she's gone. You can come back to the palace if you want to."

"You got rid of her?" Her puzzlement is still evident as our tears dry up.

"Uhhh. Evalyn tried to kill me actually," I reply sheepishly.

"SHE WHAT?" ·

"Well, you see," I begin.

"Maybe you should sit back down for this, Harry," Ambrose suggests. I reluctantly let Trudy go and return to my seat.

"You see, I decided it was time—past-time, actually—to take control of my life and do what I want." I cover Ambrose's hand on the table with my own, holding on tightly to reassure myself that he is here. "I chose to tell the court, and the kingdom, that I am gay."

"Really?" Trudy asks.

"Yes. Evalyn didn't take it well."

Ambrose scoffs. "That's an understatement."

"She tried to kill me in front of my advisors. Joseph stopped her before she could touch me, and Ambrose was there too. She is gone, Trudy. She died trying to kill me."

Without words, Ika reaches over, scooping Trudy up and nestling her in his lap. "I got you, Darlin'."

"I-I I shouldn't be so relieved," she sobs.

"You are allowed to be, Darlin'. Your largest burden is gone. It's okay to feel this way." He holds her, soothing her and whispering in her ear.

"Do you want to stay for dinner?" Ika asks over Trudy's shoulder once she is calm.

"We'd love to," Ambrose replies.

Chapter Seventeen

AMBROSE

I sit, watching Trudy and Harry discuss the past. It is going better than I hoped. She's only been able to learn so much about the palace business from Ika and myself.

"Father had a heart attack, and Mother changed after that. I think the combination of losing you and him within the year had a profound effect on her. She was a peculiar woman. I would like to say that she missed you both, but I feel that she was more about how her public perception would be affected as a queen with a missing daughter and no king," Harry says.

"I know I should feel sad, and I suppose I do to an extent. No matter what happened, they were my family," Trudy replies.

Harry is absorbed in her, hanging on every word. I realise they have never had a conversation like this before. It was always cold and snarky between them.

"Sadly, I feel nothing," she continues. "Not relief, not sadness. It's just no longer relevant to me. I spent so long doing anything they wanted from me, and now I only have to think of me. I am my own priority for once in my life, and I cannot tell you how good it feels. In the last two days, my Ika has taught me to embrace who I am. He also taught me how to light a fire and break out of a cell."

We all laughed at the cell break comment.

Trudy looks over to where Ika stands in the kitchen, preparing dinner. "He saw me, not the princess, not a bitch, but me. He loves me for who I am. I cannot regret anything I have been through as it brought me to him." Trudy stands and walks over to Ika, wrapping her arms around him and pressing herself into his back.

"I do love you, Darlin'," Ika says, dropping the knife he was using to prepare the food. He holds her hands against his chest.

"I love you too, Ika."

"You are staying," Harry states. I know he was hoping to have her come home with us.

"I am," Trudy answers, not realising he wasn't asking her – not anymore.

Harry turns to me. "I love you, Ro."

My smile is so bright I could blind him. "I love you too, Baby."

"You'll come home with me?" he asks tentatively. I know we will both need reassurances for a while; everything that happened between us won't go away overnight.

"Yes, Harry. I'm not leaving this time. You are stuck with me now." I lean in and place a soft kiss against his lips. He whimpers as I pull back, wanting more. I laugh and look over to Trudy and Ika in the kitchen. "Not with an audience," I whisper.

Ika resumes cooking, and Trudy helps him prepare the table. I am surprised they made enough for Joseph and the two guards outside and invite them in to join us for dinner, lamb chops with a variety of fresh vegetables that Ika grew himself. It's something that my father would never have considered. As we all sit down for dinner, I know this will be normal for us now. We will come here for a family dinner, or they will come to us. This relationship needs a lot of work and repair, but we will start here.

"Trudy," Ika began once we had finished dinner, "I know that you originally decided to stay with me to get away from the palace."

"Ika—"

"No, Darlin', please let me say this." He pauses and waits for her to nod before continuing. "Evalyn is gone, and Harrison is here to repair his relationship with you. You have the world at your fingertips, and you do not have to stay here any longer."

"This is my home Ika."

Ika laughs. "I know Darlin', and I ain't trying to kick you out. I am trying to say we can travel together if you want to."

"You are?"

"I know you felt trapped in the palace, and I would like to help you on your next adventure. Show you where I have been and discover new places together."

"And prevent you from getting lost again," Harry interjects, causing Trudy to chuckle.

"I would love that, Ika."

"I know we have only known each other for a few days, but nothing in my life has ever felt more natural—more perfect. I would like to marry you." Ika turns to Harry, "If that's okay?"

"I don't think that's up to me, mate," Harry replies jokingly, and we all turn back to Trudy.

"So, Trudy, will you marry me?" Ika asks her.

Trudy's eyes are as wide as our dinner plates as she sits there silently staring at Ika.

"You don't have to," He backpedals at her silence. "I love you, and we can still travel and live here. If you don't want to marry me, that's..." Trudy's squeal cuts him off. She flings herself at Ika, crawling into his lap and attacks his face with kisses.

"Of." Kiss. "Course." Kiss. "I'll." Kiss. "Marry you." Kiss. "You dingbat." Kiss.

EPILOGUE

Harrison

"I cannot believe he proposed," I say to Ambrose, rolling over and snuggling into his side. After dinner, we travelled back to the palace and fell into bed.

"Why?"

"Don't mistake me, Ambrose, I am happy for her. They seem happy and well suited. They only just met, though."

"They are lucky to be able to claim what they want straight away. If things had been different, I would have proposed to you years ago."

"You would have?"

"Actually..." He trails off, rolling away from me and getting out of bed.

"Where are you going?" I ask, my eyes raking over his naked form. He retreats to where he dropped his clothes earlier, rifling through them until he finds something and returns to the edge of the bed.

"Harrison," Ambrose says, kneeling, holding a ring out to me, "You are my lover, my past and my future. Will you give me the greatest honour and become my husband?"

"Oh, Ro." I gasped. "Yes."

He tackles me back on the bed, kissing me deeply.

I pull back and look into his eyes, laughing lightly, "I think I am supposed to be the one to ask you, as the king and all. Oh my God, that's it!"

"What's it?"

"At Trudy and Ika's, there was something off, and I couldn't place it. I just realised what was different. Neither of them treated me as above them or as a king. They treated me as an equal, as a brother." Warmth fills me. I felt at peace for the first time in forever. Things were finally looking up.

"They did, Baby. That okay with you?"

"That's perfect for me," I whisper back. I kiss my future husband, rolling him underneath me.

"If someone told me a week ago that I would have you in my bed, and Trudy back, I would have said it was impossible."

"Yet here we are," he leans up, kissing my neck.

"And here you will stay," I whisper, claiming his mouth, his body as mine. "You really want to become 'King Consort?'" I chuckle.

"I have never wanted anything but you, Baby."

THE END

ACKNOWLEDGMENTS

Thank you again to everyone who helped make this book happen.

My darling Hayden, thank you for your support, encouragement, and ability to put up with me. You are an amazing man and I will forever be grateful to have found my own novel worthy romance with you.

Thank you to Isabou, Bec and Bronwyn for helping me vet out this book and beta reading for me. You helped me so much in the creative progress and motivating me to continue writing.

A huge shout out to Cameron, Lea Anne and Erin from Salt & Sage Books for your friendship and editing services supporting me in this endeavor.

Thank you to my readers who read my first book, The Princess and The Lumberjack and gave me the encouragement to keep writing.

A thank you will never be enough; but to my parents, and in-laws —Adele, Martin, Treena, Cathie and Jeff—I would not be the person that I am without you all in my life. You have each had a hand in shaping who I am, without all of you none of this would be possible.

Also, to my writing buddies and fur babies, Amber and Daisy, your love keeps me sane.

Heidi grew up in south-west Sydney, Australia, and now lives in the Southern Highlands of NSW with her marvellous boyfriend, Hayden. Heidi is a dog mum to two beautiful, attention loving girls, Amber and Daisy. Heidi is 24 and has 2 brothers and a sister, and is a part of a crazy *Brady Bunch* family.

Heidi had difficulties learning and maintaining the standard literacy and numeracy requirements in school, until she found her love for reading. It all started with a cringe worthy obsession over a certain Edward Cullen, which has fuelled Heidi to go on to reading 200+ books a year.

With a passion for reading, Heidi began writing short stories, and has always had an overactive imagination. Heidi comes across as a loud, boisterous person, who is actually a shy girl terrified of rejection. This fear held Heidi captive for a long time and prevented Heidi from sharing any of her writing - until June 2020 when she released her first book – The Princess and The Lumberjack.

Please contact Heidi, or leave any reviews and feedback, she would love to hear from you and what you think of her work.